# Felic...

She sta... 
torture...
hard, s...
surprised.

Lowering his head, he kissed her gently. She didn't close her eyes. She realized then she'd just made love with a stranger. *On her wedding night.*

Nick noticed her wariness. "Are you all right?"

"Uh, yes."

He frowned. His expression, his body language told her he didn't believe her. She'd better reassure him—or there would be trouble.

"I hope it was okay for you," she said, attempting to be lighthearted.

"How could it not be?"

It was an ambiguous response. Was he saying sex was sex? Or was he saying she was absolutely fabulous?

She looked at him to try to gauge his response, and was surprised to find him glaring at her. "You did your job, if that's what you're worried about. Very, very well." Nick stalked off to the bathroom.

Felicia lay still, staring at the ceiling. The tears came slowly, but the pain was much quicker. Now she knew what it *really* meant to be Nick Mondavi's wife.

Dear Reader,

I suppose everyone has their special passions in life. Mine are simple—I love to write and I love to cook. So naturally I enjoyed writing *Just Desserts*. You'll find my favorite recipes at the end of the book.

As with many of my stories, there is a bit of personal history behind the recipes, too. One of my earliest editors at Harlequin was, like me, a confirmed chocaholic. After discussing with me the relative merits of dark chocolate over milk chocolate, she sent me the recipe for the mousse, and I've been making it for over ten years now.

My stepchildren's favorite dessert growing up was the chocolate cream cheese brownies. And Matthew and Sybil still love it when I send them a batch. But my husband's personal favorite is the Italian Wedding Cake. Ronn *loves* coconut. I made this cake for him the first time he came to my place for dinner. He was hooked. A year and a half later I gave the recipe to the caterer, who made the cake at our wedding. And, like Felicia and Nick, that cake was the start of something wonderful.

Happy eating!

*Janice Kaiser*

# Janice Kaiser
# JUST DESSERTS

# Harlequin Books

TORONTO • NEW YORK • LONDON
AMSTERDAM • PARIS • SYDNEY • HAMBURG
STOCKHOLM • ATHENS • TOKYO • MILAN
MADRID • WARSAW • BUDAPEST • AUCKLAND

For Carolyn and Robert Buchanan,
who love desserts as much as I do.

ISBN 0-373-25706-6

JUST DESSERTS

# Prologue

"YOUR BROTHER is dead six months, dying for his country. My oldest son. Gone. I got nobody left but you, Carlo," she said. "And now this. How could you? Haven't I suffered enough?"

"Mama, it was an accident. I swear to you."

Carlo Mauro watched his mother pacing back and forth next to the wheezing boiler in the basement of the tenement building, his eyes welling with tears. Three weeks before the truce brought an end to the fighting in Korea, his brother had been killed. Since then, he had lived under the shroud of his mother's sorrow. And now he'd brought her more pain.

"It wasn't my fault," Carlo lamented. "Joey pulls a knife on me. What do you want me to do? Let him cut me?"

"You shouldn't be with people like Joey," she shot back. "I tell you not to go with people like him, and look what you got! You fight over dice, you kill a boy, and now your life is ruined!"

"It's not ruined, Mama. I'll go away. I'll leave New York."

"Sure. And how far do you think you'll get? The police will have you before you get to New Jersey. I don't got no money to give you, Carlo. You're nineteen years old. How you going to live? Every policeman in the United States is looking for you."

"It was self-defense."

"Who's going to believe you? Nobody, that's who!"

Carlo put his head in his hands. For two days he'd hidden in the basement of his grandmother's building, afraid to go home, afraid to be on the street. Finally, Nonna had called his mother to come over. She'd been real careful because the cops were out looking for him, but she hadn't been followed. When she saw him she'd held him in her arms and kissed him and cried. Then she'd hit him on the side of the head for disgracing the family and his dead father's name.

His mother stopped pacing. She put her hands on her hips and stared at him with hard, sharp eyes. "If I give you to the police, you will spend the next twenty years in prison, which I can't do."

Carlo felt his stomach clench. He searched his mother's eyes. "So, what are you going to do, Mama?"

"I'm taking you to Mr. Antonelli. I'm going to ask him to help."

"What for? Vinny Antonelli won't help me," Carlo wailed. "The Mafia doesn't care about people like us."

"He might not help you, Carlo, but maybe he'll help me." Her lips pressed into a thin line. "When I was seventeen, I knew Vincent Antonelli's older brother, Frederico. It was before your father. We all lived in the same neighborhood. Freddy wanted to marry me, but I said no because I didn't love him. This hurt him so bad that when I married your father, Frederico killed himself. Vincent was only a boy at the time, but he said to me when we passed in the street, 'You'll be sorry some day.' That's all he said. Now I must go to him and say he was right, that I should have married his brother."

"What good will it do?"

"Pride is an important thing in a man. Even men like Vinny Antonelli have honor—their own kind, yes, but it is honor."

As CARLO and his mother walked through the snowy streets of Brooklyn, he pulled his hat down low over his eyes. The collar of his topcoat was turned up. They didn't pass any policemen, but when they saw a young soldier, probably just back from Korea, he felt ashamed. His mother said nothing, but he knew she was thinking about Tony.

When they came to the café where Vincent Antonelli ran his business, Carlo felt his blood run cold. He'd heard about men who had turned to Antonelli for help. Nobody was the same afterward. There were stories of cruelty, even death, for those who crossed the neighborhood capo, made deals they couldn't keep. Seeing Vinny was always a last resort.

A dangerous-looking man who acted as if he'd never smiled in his life opened the door for Carlo and his mother. "Wait here," he commanded before disappearing into a back room that was cut off from the main café by a drape covering an arched doorway.

Carlo was nervous. He looked around the room at the men fingering their wineglasses, watching them. The man without the smile reappeared, signaling for them to follow by crooking his finger. They stepped through the doorway into a smoky back room. Vinny Antonelli was seated at a round table. The glass of red wine in front of him glowed like a ruby in the light from the lamp hanging above his head.

Vinny was thirty. He wore a black suit and white tie, his dark hair neatly parted, his close-shaved face blue-black along his jaw and over the three-inch scar that cut diagonally across his chin. Carlo had seen him in the street a few times, usually getting into or out of his big Buick sedan, but he'd never looked into his eyes before. It was a frightening experience.

Antonelli stared blankly at them for a moment, then gestured with a hand that held a big, smoking cigar. "It's been a long time, Rosa. They tell me there is something you want."

As Carlo watched, his mother went to the table and knelt at Vincent Antonelli's feet. She proceeded to humble herself as if she were in a confessional, speaking to a priest.

Carlo listened mutely as his mother explained the family's problem and tearfully pleaded for help. When she'd finished, she sobbed quietly, still on her knees, her head bowed.

Antonelli let her cry for a time, drawing on his cigar and blowing smoke toward the ceiling. Then he looked at Carlo, who swallowed hard, wanting to cry himself.

"Carlo," Antonelli said, "why are you standing there while your poor mother begs for your life. Be a good son. Come be by your mother."

Carlo stumbled forward. He knelt beside his mother, barely able to look Vincent Antonelli in the eye. The capo drew on his cigar and blew more smoke into the air. He stared at his wineglass, but did not touch it.

"My brother loved your mother very much, Carlo," Antonelli said. "You could very easily be his son."

Carlo lowered his eyes. He was so nervous he was afraid his bladder would burst and he'd disgrace himself.

"My brother was a very forgiving man," Antonelli went on. "I think he'd want me to be forgiving, too. Which means you are a very lucky boy." Vinny puffed on his cigar. "Would you like my help, Carlo?"

Carlo nodded dumbly.

"Fine. But there is one small thing. Every kindness has its price, just as every insult has its punishment. If I help you, then you will owe me a favor. I am doing you a big kindness, so the favor you owe me will be very great. Do you understand?"

"Yes, Mr. Antonelli."

"You say yes, but I'm not sure you do. Let me explain this way. I am going to give you your life. A new life. Somewhere else. Maybe California. Your problems here will be behind you, but you will owe me, Carlo. You will owe me your life."

"What do you want me to do, Mr. Antonelli?"

The capo drew on his cigar. Then, smiling faintly, he shook his head. "I don't know."

"Carlo will do anything you say," his mother said.

"Is that true?" Antonelli asked.

Carlo nodded. "Yes, it is true."

"Then I will count on that. It may not be soon, Carlo. It will be when I need a favor, something as important to me as your life is to you. But when I ask, I expect you to give."

Carlo nodded again.

"Then I have your word?" Antonelli said. "On the head of your mother you will swear to do what I ask, no matter what, no matter when?"

"Yes, Mr. Antonelli. I promise on the life of my mother."

"Good, Carlo. You're a good boy. Now kiss your mother. You won't see her again for many years. Maybe never."

Carlo swallowed hard. He turned to his mother, whose face was streaked with tears. He kissed her on the cheek and glanced at Vinny Antonelli, whose heavy-lidded eyes were dark and expressionless.

"Be glad you have such a loving mother," he said flatly. "You owe her. And you owe me, Carlo. You owe me your life. Don't forget, because I won't. Someday the debt will be repaid."

It's my mistake that did not pay you but let me double-
take care. Mayor O'duratta... Your problems here
with I defend you, not trust a high-
me to do not want us to do that...with...
...hitting Philly he

## 1

SHE STARED at the fishing boat pitching and rolling in the waves a half a mile off Ocean Beach. Earlier she'd watched a freighter inch its way up the coast toward Portland or Seattle or Alaska. But it was gone now. Out of sight.

Felicia Mauro turned her attention to the surf fifty yards from where she and her mother sat in beach chairs, whiling away a lazy Monday afternoon as her father stood at water's edge, fishing. She watched as he lay the tip of the pole on the sand behind him before whipping it forward and sending his baited hook far out beyond the crashing waves.

"Has Jonah caught his whale yet?" her mother asked, rousing herself from her nap.

"No, but he's trying."

Louisa tucked the blanket around her legs. "For all the years I'm married to the man, he never goes fishing once," she said. "And now that's all he wants to do when he's not in the restaurant. Fish, fish, fish. When he does catch something, neither of us would eat it. 'Let the poor fish stay in the ocean,' I tell him. But no, he has to come to the beach and throw a line into the water."

Felicia stared at the back of her dear father, his fedora pulled down low over his ears, the brim turned up comically, his trouser legs rolled to his knees, exposing his spindly legs. She pulled her thick green sweater around her neck. It was July, but July in San Francisco could be as cold as January in a lot of places, especially if there was a stiff ocean breeze.

"One day I asked him," her mother went on, "Carlo, why fishing after all these years? And you know what he says to me? That when he was a boy in Brooklyn he would go to Rockaway Beach and watch the old men fish while him and his friends would drink beer. He laughed at them, he said, and now that he's an old man he wants to fish and know what it feels like."

Felicia smiled at the notion. Her poor sweet dad. His heart attack six months earlier had really changed him. Almost overnight he'd become sentimental, melancholy and fragile. He'd even talked about New York, and heaven knows, he'd never spoken about his past before. It was as though his life didn't start until he'd arrived in San Francisco and began working in a North Beach restaurant as a busboy. That was forty years ago.

"But I'm glad for the fishing," Louisa said, "he seems more at peace. For that, I'll sit here in the sand, bundled up like an Eskimo."

"Pop has always worked too hard. He's devoted himself to the restaurant. It's been his life."

"Except for you, Felicia. You've been his joy." There was a pause. "And his sorrow."

Felicia rolled her eyes. It was clear what her mother was referring to—Felicia had turned thirty-five in May and there was no prospect of marriage. And what was most confounding to her parents, she had no desire for a husband, either.

Well, that wasn't entirely accurate. She loved children and knew there'd be none without a husband, but that meant finding a man, and none of them interested her— at least none had for a long, long time.

"I know you don't like to hear it," her mother said, not willing to let the conversation drop, "but what Italian man wants to die without grandchildren?"

"Mama, please don't start in on me," Felicia said, laying back against the beach chair. The wind was flavored with a salty mist. She gazed at the hazy profile of the Farallon Islands on the horizon.

"Am I wrong?" her mother asked. "Your father can't help how he feels. Now that he's had his heart trouble, he asks me all the time, 'Do you think Felicia will find a man? Will I have grandchildren?'"

Felicia groaned. "Pops knows perfectly well what happened, so why does he say something like that?"

"Because everybody needs somebody, Felicia."

"Aunt Cecilia never had a man in her life, and she's happy."

"My sister is a nun."

"So? Can't there be anything besides the church and men for a woman to care about?"

"Yes, children."

"Oh, Mama, why can't you and Pops let me live my life the way I want to live it?"

"Because we love you."

Felicia fell silent. How could she tell her mother she'd already tried to care for someone, but couldn't? How could she explain that the pain of trying and failing was worse even than not having someone? True, she wasn't the only woman who'd been jilted, but that didn't mean she had to make herself do something she didn't want to do just because people expected it.

"All right, so you don't want to hear another lecture," her mother said. "But let me ask you one last thing. If your father had a friend who had a son—"

"Mama!"

"No, listen to me, Felicia, please. It's not what you think. This is not a boy. He is a man. Forty-eight, maybe fifty. He is a doctor. His wife died two years ago. He is lonely. He has two sons who need a mother."

"Stop right there, Mama. I don't want to be a substitute wife and mother. Codependency is the last thing I need."

"Codependency? What's this? The man is a doctor. He has a nice house in Pacific Heights. He's a little heavy around the middle, but he's not fat. He has nice eyes, like my father."

"Mama!"

"Would it hurt if he comes to dinner?"

The wind whipped Felicia's mahogany-colored hair across her face. She pulled the strands from her eyes, green eyes like her mother's. They stared at each other for a long time.

"If I agree and nothing comes of it, then it will only make Pops sadder," Felicia said. "Why get his hopes up for nothing?"

"Because hope is all he has."

The wind stung her eyes, making them water. The wrenching emotion inside her turned the water to tears. Felicia wiped her cheeks with the sleeve of her sweater and sighed deeply.

"Here," her mother said, snatching up her purse, "I have a picture of him. His name is Carl, like your father!"

While her mother searched for the photo, Felicia watched her father reeling in his line. Then he leaned down to get more bait from his bucket. As he secured a chunk of fish on his hook, her mother thrust a glossy photo into her hands.

Felicia studied the picture without much interest. Carl, a portly man in shirtsleeves and tie, stood between two gangly boys. All three had the same grin. Carl wore thick horn-rimmed glasses, so it was difficult to tell what he really looked like. A deep sadness went through her. Her mother seemed to notice.

"He's not so heavy now, according to his father," Louisa said. "Maybe ten or fifteen pounds lighter."

"Has he seen a picture of me?"

Her mother lowered her eyes. "Yes. Of course, he thinks you're beautiful, because you are. 'How could such a gorgeous woman be without a husband?' is what he said to your father."

"What did Pops say?"

Her mother shrugged. "That you are particular. What can he say? That you were left at the altar and haven't recovered?"

"The truth is the truth," Felicia said.

"Of course, but why tell a man something that is not important?"

"I am who I am, Mama."

"Yes, and you are a lovely girl, inside and out."

Felicia knew it would be a terrible mistake to humor her parents, but she felt herself caving in. And not for the first time—though for the last few years potential suitors hadn't found their way to the Mauro dinner table. Obviously, her father's illness had changed that.

She sighed. God knew, she wasn't going to marry someone just to make her parents happy. On the other hand, it was probably selfish to deny her father hope. And one dinner wasn't much to ask.

"Okay," she said, "I'll come. But only one dinner. I won't promise more."

Louisa reached over and took her daughter's hand. "Thank you, Felicia. Thank you for your father's sake. You're a good daughter. God will bless you."

# 2

NICK MONDAVI stepped out of the taxi in the East Side neighborhood he'd visited only two or three times in the last ten years. He paid the driver and turned to study the park where the meeting was to take place. From his vantage point, he could see the sandy area where preschoolers played while their mothers or nannies idled away the late morning hours. It was a mild, balmy July day.

Nick began walking around the park as the cries of children competed with the remote sounds of the city—traffic on Canal Street, a siren wailing in the direction of the Manhattan Bridge, the rear doors of a delivery truck slamming shut across the street. It was an innocuous neighborhood at the edge of Little Italy, more Chinese than Italian. So far as Nick was aware, it had no particular connection to anything, which was probably why Uncle Vinny had picked it.

About halfway along the west side of the park Nick saw a man leaning against the fender of a shiny black sedan that was parked next to a fire hydrant. The man, burly and malevolent-looking, watched him approach without moving. When Nick was within twenty feet or so, the man casually gestured toward the park, indicating the way Nick should go.

That was the way Uncle Vinny did things. Nick wasn't surprised. But he'd been curious about what was going on ever since he'd gotten the message that his uncle needed to talk to him. They hadn't had three face-to-face conversations in well over a decade. Vincent Antonelli's role in life was no secret—his name was as recognizable to most New Yorkers as the mayor's. It was not a family connection Nick was proud of, but it was a fact and he didn't hide from it, though it wasn't widely known that he was the nephew of one of New York's most feared and famous underworld figures.

Nick didn't have far to go along the path before he came to an isolated bench. Seated on it was a dapperly dressed man with silver hair, a round stomach and a faintly sad expression, which brightened slightly as Nick approached. He got to his feet.

"Nicky," the older man said, grabbing Nick affectionately by the nape of the neck with his rough hand. They embraced.

"It's good to see you, Uncle Vinny."

"Yeah, sure. Good to see me here in the bushes, away from the eyes of the world."

Nick started to reply, but Vincent Antonelli cut him off with a wave of the hand.

"You live in your world and I live in mine, Nicky. That was the promise I made to your mother on her death bed, God bless her soul." Vinny, still vigorous, though diminished by age, glanced at the bench. "Come sit and talk with me, we don't got all day. You got things to do and so do I."

Vinny sat down gingerly, dropping precipitously the last few inches. Nick was surprised by how much his uncle seemed to have aged. True, it had been years since he'd seen him, but it wasn't as if he hadn't seen pictures of the man. Photos appeared in the papers from time to time—especially when he was having trouble with the law, which had been more often in recent years. And his aunt kept pictures of Vinny around the house. Still, seeing a man in the flesh was always more telling.

Maria Antonelli had been separated from Vinny for more than three decades but, being a good Catholic, she refused to divorce him. Vinny had always had other women in his life, so the lady he'd been keeping company with at the time of their split wasn't the cause of the breakup. Maria had just come to the end of her rope. She was tired of pretending that she lived a normal life. Vinny had to get out of the mob or out of the house. He got out of the house, but he didn't abandon his wife or his daughters. He simply provided for them in absentia.

Nick had been away in an exclusive private school when his aunt and uncle—who'd raised him from infancy—had gone their separate ways. If anything, the estrangement had made it easier for Vinny to keep his promise to Nick's mother to give him a life away from organized crime.

"You know, Nicky," the old man said, running his finger over the diagonal scar on his chin, "I always did my best to see you was taken care of. You went to the best schools. I gave money through your aunt so you could start your business, the same as all the blue blood Harvard boys you went to school with."

"I know, Uncle Vinny. You've never been less than generous to me."

"Well, I promised your mother I'd see you had a good life, Nicky, and that's what I done. But I'm not here to ask thanks. I'm here because we got a problem."

Nick heard a serious turn in Vincent Antonelli's voice, a turn that he'd recognized to be ominous from the time he was just a kid. "What sort of problem?"

"It seems the Feds have decided they're going to make war on us, real war. The heat's been on a couple of years. Nothing new in that. But I've got ears inside the Feds that tells me what's up and word's come down they're going after us big time. Worse, they're coming after our families."

Vincent Antonelli took a cigar out of his pocket and lit it with a gold lighter. He puffed on it a few times to make sure it was burning well. He blew a cloud of smoke toward the sky. "I don't imagine you've been served with a warrant, have you?"

Nick blinked. "A warrant?"

"Yeah, the invitation they write themselves to take apart your business."

"I know what a warrant is, Uncle Vinny. Why would they serve a warrant on me?"

"Because you're family, Nicky."

"But I haven't done anything that would cause the government to investigate me," Nick protested.

"That doesn't make any difference. You're related to me, that's all they need."

Nick shifted uneasily. "Well, they can investigate all they want. I haven't done anything illegal."

"It's not quite so simple," Vinny said, exhaling cigar smoke into the summer air.

"What do you mean?"

"There's two things you don't know." Vinny put his hand on Nick's arm in a gesture of apology. "And I'm sorry you have to hear about them this way, believe me."

He cleared his throat. "First, that money I gave you to get started. There wasn't no trust from your mother, like I told you. It was from me. I gave it in her name because that's what she would have wanted. Now, as you can imagine, the Feds don't like my money, which means they don't like your money."

"But you gave me that hundred thousand fifteen years ago. It's been turned over a dozen times since then."

"The Feds don't forget, Nicky." He drew on his cigar. "But that's only the start. We got bigger problems. Something else."

Nick was afraid to ask. Already he was feeling sick. He'd never approved of what his uncle did, in fact he'd hated it. But Uncle Vinny had done at least one thing that was honorable—he had kept his family away from his work. Vinny had never demanded that they accept him. He'd never insisted on validation. Nick's aunt was a decent woman who had done her best to instill sound morals and values in her nephew and her daughters. And Vinny, to his credit, had not interfered.

"You see," Vinny went on, "when I brought you and Maria here from the old country, I made a bad mistake. I never got you the right papers. Since I'd come in illegally years before, I tried winking at the law. I thought I'd fixed it later, but I didn't. The immigration people have been digging the last few months and they're onto us."

"Wait a minute, Uncle Vinny. Are you saying I'm not a citizen, that my papers were faked?"

"Unfortunately, Nicky."

"But that can't be! I've lived in this country since I was six months old. I've gone through the naturalization process. I've got a passport, everything."

"My lawyers say they can undo all that if they find there's been fraud."

Nick felt as though the wind had just been kicked out of him. He couldn't believe what he was hearing.

"I know this is comin' as a surprise," Vinny said, obviously embarrassed. "It's my fault. I take full responsibility. And I swear to you, Nicky, I'm going to make it right."

Nick Mondavi put his head in his hands. He suddenly had a pounding headache. He'd heard about former Nazis being thrown out of the country, their citizenship stripped after forty years or more of living as Americans. But this was different. He was no war criminal. He wasn't even a street criminal. He was a businessman, a real estate developer.

"Uncle Vinny," he said, bewildered, "I can't believe the government would come after me. Even if they do, I should be able to beat whatever they throw at me in court."

"Don't count on it. They think you're laundering for me. They won't be able to prove it, because it's not true, but that won't stop them from pushing what they have—the immigration thing. If they can't get you for whackin' a wise guy, they get you for tax evasion. It's the way the Feds are. Either way, they clean you out and your reputation is in shreds."

"So what do I do about it?"

"That's why I'm here, Nicky. I got a plan."

Anything Vinny had in mind would be unsavory—Nick would bet his life on that much. He sighed, knowing his uncle was no fool, that the problem was indeed serious if it had come to this. Resignation enveloped him like a shroud. "What's your plan, Uncle Vinny?" he asked quietly.

"First thing is, you need a wife. You have a girlfriend?"

"A girlfriend? You mean a fiancée, don't you?"

"Yeah, somebody you like, somebody you'd marry."

Nick shook his head, a queasy feeling going through him. "I'm sort of between women at the moment, Uncle Vinny."

"You don't got *nobody*? A good-looking boy like you? Hell, with your face I could do better than Sinatra when he was young. And it's not like you don't got money or you're a drug addict or somethin'."

"Even if I'm desperate," Nick said, shaking his head, "I can't take some woman out to dinner and then propose marriage."

Vinny ignored his comment. "You could buy a wife, of course—money can buy anything—but you gotta be careful. You can't get no tramp. You need somebody legit, a classy broad from a good family. Otherwise the Feds won't buy it."

"You're saying if I'm respectably married, I'm safe?"

"No, but you're better off. My *consigliari* have been lookin' into the matter. Concerning a wife, it's got to be someone American-born. And it wouldn't hurt if you had a kid."

"Hey, we're jumping ahead of ourselves, aren't we, Uncle Vinny? You're talking about a kid and the only woman in my life at the moment is somebody I've taken to dinner twice. And she's a mortgage banker, somebody I took out for business reasons as much as for pleasure."

"Be careful of bankers. Better you find a nice family girl—somebody who cooks and changes diapers. Someone like Gina, God rest her soul."

They observed a moment of silence. That same sick feeling went through Nick that always came when Gina was mentioned.

"Girls from the old country make better wives," Vinny said, "but you can't get another immigrant. You need a real American girl, born and bred."

Nick decided this had gone on long enough. It was time he took charge. "Look, Uncle Vinny, I don't know why we're discussing this. If I'm served, I'll get a lawyer and fight it all the way to the Supreme Court, if I have to. I haven't done anything wrong. I know justice doesn't always prevail, but as far as I'm concerned, it's my best chance."

Vincent Antonelli shook his head. "You don't understand what we're up against. It's not just your citizenship, Nicky. They'll take your business. Fortunately, because of ears I got inside the Feds, I know what's comin' down. We got time. But if you don't listen to me, they will pick you clean, then ship you outta here. I know what I'm talkin' about. So the least you can do is hear me out."

If Nick knew one thing about his uncle, it was that Vincent Antonelli was not a man to borrow trouble. The fact that he'd asked for this meeting meant the danger was real and immediate. "Okay," Nick said with a sigh. "What do you want me to do?"

"First, you got to liquidate your real estate and put the money offshore. Nothing illegal in that. I can even provide clean buyers. No dirty money."

"Let me think about that."

"Second, we got to find you a respectable wife."

"You going to scour the lonely hearts columns for me, Uncle Vinny?"

Vincent Antonelli took Nick's jaw in his hand, squeezing it firmly, the way he did when Nick was six. "Listen to me, Nicky, and listen good. I'm coming here at great risk. I want to save your ass because you're my blood and I promised your mother I'd look after you to my dying day. I never break a promise."

"Uncle Vinny," Nick said, pulling away, "I'm thirty-eight now, not twelve. I don't think this is what my mother had in mind when she got you to make that promise."

"Look, you got problems now because I screwed up. If they deport you, strip you to your shorts, it's on my head. So I'm going to find you a wife who won't give you no trouble. A nice girl from a good family who'll keep her mouth shut. That's not easy to find. Even if you got a wife who loves you, there is no guarantee she will stick by you unless she's got another reason besides your pretty face and your wallet. *Capisce?*"

"Uncle Vinny—"

"If you don't like who I get for you, dump her when this is over," Vincent Antonelli said, cutting him off. "But don't look down your nose at me just because I ain't been to Harvard. Maybe I know what's best."

Nick's jaw clenched. He had Antonelli blood in him, too. In his case, passions played out differently, but it didn't mean he didn't have pride.

He counted to ten, recalling his aunt claiming that the best way to handle Vinny was to give him his head and then find other, subtler ways to influence him. This was much more than a battle of wills. Vincent Antonelli's sacred duty was at issue. Even if the man lived outside the law, he did believe in family. As Aunt Maria often said, "Even the devil was once an angel of the Lord."

"Uncle Vinny," Nick said, "I know you've got my interests at heart, and I appreciate it. But I wouldn't be a man if I didn't decide what to do for myself. I owe you a chance to help, but in the long run I'll do what I have to do."

Vincent Antonelli nodded. He gripped Nick by the nape of the neck again and gave him an affectionate squeeze. "You got your grandfather's blood in your veins, Nicky. I knew it." He pointed at him with his cigar. "And that's no disrespect to your father's people. But you're the son of the Antonellis."

"How, exactly, are you proposing we find the right woman, Uncle Vinny?"

Vincent Antonelli cleared his throat and glanced around. Lowering his voice he said, "I knew you been havin' problems here," he said, tapping his heart, "because of Gina dying while havin' her baby. So I already been workin' on this. It's too soon to say what I got, but it shouldn't take long to find the right girl. Give me a week and I'll have a name. The buyers for your buildings I already got, so that part you can start on right away."

He glanced around at the bushes, and Nick did, as well. Lord, he was already feeling paranoid. This was just the sort of thing he'd spent his life trying to avoid.

"Problem is, I can't be calling you up and giving you phone numbers," Vinny said. "So what I'm going to do is run everything through Maria. You can bet her phones are tapped, same as mine, but it don't look so funny if a boy talks to his aunt about women. Even the Feds expect that. So, next word you hear will be from her. But remember, whatever she says is really comin' from me. Promise me you'll listen and do what I say."

"I promise I'll keep an open mind, Uncle Vinny, but that's the best I can do."

Vincent Antonelli nodded, then checked his watch. Frowning, he took a drag on his cigar, pursed his lips and blew a stream of smoke heavenward. "It's a nice day, huh, Nicky?"

Nick Mondavi looked at the blue sky. "Yeah, it's a hell of a day."

"It's days like this a young fella falls in love," Vinny said as he gave Nick a playful poke in the solar plexus.

"Maybe so."

Vincent Antonelli sighed and got to his feet. Nick rose, as well. The old man offered his hand. Nick took it.

"Who knows," Vinny said, "maybe this will turn out to be a lucky day." He went up the path toward his car. He didn't have the vigor he once had, but he was still full of Antonelli vinegar.

Even so, Nick had noticed a change in the old boy. There was a sentimentality he'd never seen before. He smiled at the irony. Of all the evil things Vinny had done, the thing that seem to bother him most at the moment was the immigration fraud that now threatened Nick's citizenship. Funny how life produced such strange twists.

Nick sat down on the bench. He stared off, listening to the sound of the children nearby, and thought of Gina and the baby girl who'd died with her. It had been eight years now, but he could remember the first time he had seen Gina as if it was yesterday.

During a trip to Italy, they'd been introduced by his mother's cousin Adolpho. "This is somebody you should marry," Adolpho had said in broken English. And strangely enough, that was exactly what Nick had done— married that raven-haired girl with the soulful eyes.

For the briefest of moments he allowed himself to wonder if Antonelli lightning could strike twice in a lifetime. But then he realized how foolish a notion that was. He shook his head at the thought. Maybe he was getting old and sentimental, just like Uncle Vinny.

# 3

FOR THE NEXT FEW DAYS nothing was said about the chubby doctor from Pacific Heights, but Felicia noticed an extra bounce in her father's step. He came to the restaurant early three days in a row—the way he used to before his heart attack. He even hummed as he worked. It broke her heart.

Two or three times she came close to telling her father flat out that she had no desire to get seriously involved with anyone, but she couldn't bear the thought of bursting his bubble. In the end, she decided to split the difference between being true to herself and trying to be the daughter her father cherished. But she resolved not to allow this to become a trend. On Wednesday morning when she arrived at the restaurant, her father was already chopping vegetables, though it was officially the job of the sous chef.

After his heart attack, Carlo Mauro had promised to focus on quality control and do less physical work, but Felicia didn't rag him. Occasional hard work was good for his soul. Besides, their mornings were a special time. As she baked, they often talked.

"This is early even for you, Pops," she said, giving him a welcoming kiss.

"I woke up feeling like I could conquer the world, so naturally I came right down to attack the vegetables," he said with a wink.

"It's good to see you more like your old self."

"A man's never too old to be in love with life, honey."

Felicia turned on the ovens. Like her father—and for that matter, her mother—she was a cook extraordinaire. The Mauros were one of the city's leading culinary families, having made Carlo's the premiere spot for fine Italian cuisine.

Felicia could cook almost anything, but she especially liked desserts. For the past few years, she'd done little else besides refine her recipes. She had even thought about opening a dessert diner. That was on hold now, partly due to a lack of funds—she was adamant about financing it herself—and partly because of her father's health. Still, it remained a dream.

The first thing she did was check to see that the fruit had arrived. Given the season, she varied her dessert menu, and with kiwifruit, blueberries, strawberries, blackberries and peaches all in season, she often made individual fruit tarts. They were a nice contrast to her always popular cakes. Every once in a while she varied the menu with a mousse, homemade ice cream or Italian ices and biscotti.

Felicia was just getting ready to start making the pastry for the fruit tarts when there was a rap on the back door.

"You expecting another delivery?" she asked.

"No, everything's come that's scheduled." Carlo wiped his hands on his apron, then threw the bolt and opened the door a crack. Felicia heard a man's voice.

"Mr. Mauro, I'd like to talk, if I can have a few minutes. The name's Louie."

She didn't recognize the name, but whoever it was spoke with an accent—a New York accent not unlike her father's.

"Do I know you?" Carlo said warily.

"No, but how about lettin' me in? I'm here at the request of Vinny Antonelli."

She saw her father go white as he stepped back to let the door swing open. The man in the doorway, wearing a black sport shirt and slacks, wasn't tall, but he was built like a bulldog. His neck was as big around as his head, his arms were like railroad ties, his stubby legs could have been tree stumps. He wore a thick gold chain around his neck and had thinning black hair. He regarded them with flat eyes. When they made way for him, he entered.

Louie glanced around as if to see who else was present, then he turned to face them. "Sorry to drop in uninvited, but we got important business." He looked Felicia up and down. "Hello, Miss Mauro."

"Have we met?"

He grinned. "No, but I feel like I know you."

Felicia turned to her father. "What's this about, Pops?"

Carlo took a breath to speak, but no words came out.

"Me and your father have some things to discuss," Louie said. Again he looked around. "You got an office, Mr. Mauro?"

Felicia saw her father's lip tremble. "We can go into the restaurant," Carlo mumbled. He turned to her. "Go ahead and do your baking, honey. Don't worry."

He led Louie through the swinging doors into the main dining room. Felicia was sure something was wrong. And the name this Louie character had invoked seemed to be the key. What was it? Vinny. Yes, Vinny Something-or-other.

She crept to the swinging door and pushed it open a crack. Her father and Louie were in a booth at the front of the dining room. Her father was speaking softly, but Louie's voice was loud and carried well.

"Vinny sends his greetings to you and your family," Louie said. "He hopes I find you happy and in good health."

"Things are okay." Carlo mumbled something unintelligible, then she heard him add, "So, why are you here?"

Louie leaned back and laid his beefy arm across the top of the red leather banquette. "It's hard to know how to put this, so I'll say it out straight. Vinny wants your daughter."

Felicia gasped. Could she have heard right? She pushed the door open a bit wider and strained to hear. Her father seemed to be stunned. It took him a good minute to say anything. When he did speak, his voice was thready.

"What do you mean, he wants my daughter?"

"Vinny's had me out here checkin' on things . . . talkin' to people. Bottom line is, your daughter fits perfectly what we need. She's clean, good-looking, real nice family situation, far from New York, just what we're looking for. Vinny needs her to marry his nephew, Mr. Mauro."

Felicia couldn't believe her ears. Was this a joke?

"This is not true," Carlo muttered. "You're making this up. You want something else. Is this about money? Did Vinny decide to collect his debt? I'm too old for my life to be worth much so he's bringing in my family. Is that it?"

"No, no. Nothing like that. This is for real. Vinny's nephew needs a wife real bad and we're askin' for your daughter."

Felicia pressed against the door so hard that she nearly fell into the dining room.

"I was hopin' I wouldn't have to remind you, Mr. Mauro, but you owe Vinny your life. He didn't want me pointin' that out unless you somehow forgot, but he's made up his mind that your daughter's marryin' his nephew. Period. Your job is to get her to do it. Am I makin' myself clear, Mr. Mauro?"

"I can't do that," Carlo stammered.

Felicia's heart pounded. She was unsure what to do. Half of her wanted to barge in and demand to know what was going on. But the other half of her knew she didn't want to know—that her father wouldn't *want* her to know.

"Don't make this hard for me," Louie said. "I'm not going to say it too many times. Lots of things depend on it, starting with your ass. Am I clear?"

Carlo shook his head. "I'm not going to make my daughter marry anyone. You'll have to kill me first."

Louie lowered his voice, and Felicia could barely make out his words. "As you know, that can be arranged. But before we take such a big step, let's try a little friendly persuasion. Your daughter's a looker, Mr. Mauro, but she's what, thirty-five and no husband? She doesn't mess around none, and that's good. She's got a chance here to have a good life and marry a nice guy. Listen, this is the God's truth. Vinny's nephew, Nick, is legit. An Ivy League kind of guy. But he needs a wife real bad. Your daughter marries him, puts on a good show and everybody comes up winners. What could be better?"

"My daughter's got nothing to do with what happened forty years ago. I know I owe Vinny. If he wants my restaurant, it's his. If he's got to kill me, then tell him to do it. But he can't have Felicia."

"Listen, scumbag," Louie said, raising his voice, "there ain't no choice. You promised to do what Vinny needed when the time came. If I don't get the answer he wants by tonight, your dead body's only going to be the starting point. *Capisce?*"

Felicia gasped. This was like a scene in a terrible movie, only it was really happening. As she watched Louie slide out of the booth and head to the kitchen, she flung the door open.

"Who do you think you are, coming in here and threatening my father?" she demanded, her hands on her hips.

"This makes things simpler." As he got close to her, Louie reached out, grabbed her arm and spun her around. He took her jaw in his beefy hand and turned her toward her father. "See this face, Mr. Mauro? If you want it looking pretty tomorrow, I better get the right answer tonight. Otherwise, her mama's going to have a dead husband *and* an ugly daughter."

Giving her a shove in Carlo's direction, Louie stomped out. Felicia turned to her father, who looked as though he just seen the devil himself.

"Pops," she said, "what was all that about? Who's Vinny?"

He buried his face in his hands. "You don't want to know."

"I'm going to call the police."

"No!" Carlo said sharply.

Felicia was taken aback. "Why not?"

Again her father put his face in his hands. After a moment or two, she realized he was sobbing. Felicia put her arm around his shoulders.

"Pops, explain."

"I can't," he sobbed.

Then suddenly he stiffened and clutched his chest. Felicia saw his eyes roll back in his head, and he made a gurgling sound.

"Oh, my God," she cried.

When he fell forward onto the table, she ran to the phone and dialed 911.

IT WAS a mild heart attack. Most of the tests were completed by midafternoon. Louisa had been with her husband all day, holding his hand. Felicia, who'd said nothing to her mother about what had happened, spent her time at the restaurant once it was clear that her father wasn't in immediate danger.

Around three, when the chefs were on the job, Felicia went back to the hospital. She sent her mother out for a bite to eat and demanded that her father tell her exactly what had happened. Sedated, Carlo calmly told her the story. When he finished, tears were running down his cheeks.

Felicia kissed him, patted his hand, then went to the window. The whole thing seemed so absurd. It had taken a while for the fact to sink in, but she was a hostage to an obligation that had occurred five years before she was even born! Did she go to the police? Did she give in to the intimidation of a band of criminals? Did she have a choice?

There was so much she didn't know. But clearly her first priority was her father's health. At the very least she had to keep him safe and calm—and that meant stalling Louie. She'd pretend to go along with him for the time being. Then when she knew more, she could formulate a plan, decide what to do.

Felicia returned to her father's side.

"I'm so sorry this happened," he moaned. "You don't deserve this."

"You had no way of knowing, Pops. My guess is they're only trying to scare us," she said. "What good would it do to scar my face or break my legs?"

"Felicia, Vinny Antonelli does not make idle threats. A debt is a debt in his eyes. If I could pay him back with my life, I would, but he wants you!" Carlo sobbed. "How can I agree to that?" he asked tearfully. "How?"

Felicia kissed her father's head. "Don't worry, Pops," she said. "We'll figure something out. Don't worry."

LATER THAT NIGHT, as she lay in bed, Felicia couldn't help but wonder if she'd been overoptimistic with her father. Dealing with Louie hadn't been as simple as she'd hoped. When he had returned to the restaurant that evening, she'd told him exactly what he wanted to hear—that she'd marry Vinny's nephew if he still wanted her after they'd met. But what concerned her was that her qualification didn't seem to faze Louie a bit.

"You're a smart girl," he told her. "That's good. Better for everybody. Besides, Nicky's the kind girls dream about."

Felicia nearly choked on that one. Any man willing to let a woman be blackmailed into marrying him certainly wasn't *her* idea of a dream man.

"So what happens next?" she'd asked darkly.

"I'll let you know. In the meantime, be glad you have such good fortune."

*Good fortune.* Ha! Felicia stared at her dark ceiling. The only fortunate part of this mess thus far was that her father hadn't had a more serious heart attack. And she was determined that he wouldn't be affected by this in the future any more than was absolutely necessary.

That wouldn't be easy. Of course, there was no way to keep him from worrying. But in spite of Louie's confidence that Nick would marry her no matter what, she reasoned that if she could string the situation along until she actually met him, she might just be able to change things. After all, what man—even a desperate one— wanted an unwilling woman for a wife? And if the nephew didn't want her, then Vinny certainly wouldn't force her to marry into the family!

Felicia sighed. Ever since she'd been left at the altar, she'd had lots of practice turning men off. All she had to do now was turn off one more. And if she was successful, their problems would be over.

On that note, she fell into a deep sleep and didn't awaken until the phone roused her early the next morning.

"Be on the northeast corner of Washington Square at three this afternoon. Watch for a black limo. A gentleman wants to talk to you," the voice said without introduction.

She recognized Louie's distinctive accent. She wondered why the secretiveness. "Who is it? The nephew?"

"Don't ask questions," he said gruffly. "It's not good to talk on the phone. Be where I say and wear red."

Felicia went to work, but all the time she was cooking, she was uneasy. It would have helped if she'd known for certain that she was meeting the nephew—then she could at least think about the things she'd say and do to turn him off. As it was, she just couldn't be sure who or what she was facing.

As soon as she could, she left the restaurant and headed for the hospital. Fortunately, her mother wasn't around when she got there, so she and her father could talk freely. When he asked her about Louie she tried to be vague, assuring him that everything was under control. She only prayed that fate wouldn't make her out to be a liar.

At three that afternoon Felicia was at Washington Square, just as she'd been instructed. The only thing she had in red was a party dress she'd worn the last two Christmases. Though it was cut low, it was in good taste, thank God. Even so, wearing it on the street in July in broad daylight made her feel like some kind of street-walker.

At two minutes after the hour a limo pulled up at the curb. Felicia held her breath as the rear passenger door slowly opened. Looking in, she saw a silver-haired *signore* wearing an impeccable black suit and a silver tie with a mother-of-pearl clasp. He had a bit of a paunch, rosy cheeks and a faint smile. He was a good decade older than her father. It had to be Vincent Antonelli.

Felicia slowly exhaled. The man looked her over carefully and then signaled for her to get in next to him. Trembling, she complied.

"I'm Vinny Antonelli," he said when she'd closed the door.

"Nice to meet you," Felicia said, using politeness to mask her nervousness.

"Sorry about your papa's heart," he said as the driver smoothly pulled into the traffic. "How is he?"

She gave him a quick look to see what she could tell by his expression, but Vinny's face was blank. Felicia stared at her hands. She was much more nervous than when she'd told Louie she'd do as they asked. Vinny Antonelli was a powerful man, and she knew she'd have to be careful. Very careful. "Pops is fine. He's coming home tomorrow." In spite of her resolve, there was a trace of indignation in her voice.

"That's good. Good. Maybe Louie was too harsh. For that I apologize."

Felicia said nothing.

Vinny glanced out at the city as they drove. "You know, Felicia, you are the only girl for whom I've ever flown across the United States just to have a little conversation," he said.

"I'm flattered, Mr. Antonelli."

"This is a very important thing to me. I care very much about finding the right wife for my nephew. And seeing you, I'm more convinced than ever that you are the one."

That was the last thing she wanted to hear. "Do you mean because my father owes you a favor from forty years ago?" She couldn't keep the bitterness out of her voice.

"I know this has not been easy," he said, touching her arm. "For that, I am very sorry. You are correct when you say you are here because you are your father's daughter. But that is also why you will be paid for your sacrifice."

"Paid?"

"Yes, you will get two hundred fifty thousand for marrying my nephew and another hundred thousand if you have his child."

Felicia's mouth dropped open. "Nobody said anything about having a baby."

Vincent Antonelli shrugged. "That's between you and Nicky. But the hundred thousand says I think it's a good idea."

She was stunned. From the first she'd been afraid to consider what they wanted from her—exactly what they expected—because it had been so much easier to assume they were talking about a marriage of convenience. But apparently they wanted her to have a *real* marriage with this Nicky, have his children, the works.

"Don't look so unhappy," Vinny remarked. "You could do worse, believe me. Nicky's a good boy. Successful. Smart. Handsome. Most women would be glad for a husband like him."

"Perhaps. But I can't help but wonder what kind of man would want a woman who has to be blackmailed into marrying him."

"Blackmail is not a word I like. You are a girl who loves her father and worries for his health. I respect that," Vinny said. "Nick does not know the details of our arrangement, and I intend to keep it that way. You will not tell him about your father's obligation. It is our secret."

There it was. The threat. As the words sank in, Felicia felt a shroud of resignation envelop her. If she wanted to save her father, she had to do exactly what this man wanted—or at least make him think she was doing what he wanted. "You're saying you want me to lie to your nephew?"

He shrugged. "It would be nice if there was time for him to love you, and for you to love him, but there isn't."

"Then what *do* you want me to tell him? That I was bought?" There was an edge of stridency in her tone, but she couldn't help it. She felt more and more trapped by the minute.

"If necessary, you can say there was an inducement to marry him on such short notice, yes," he said, pulling an envelope out of his coat pocket. "Nicky will be practical. And you must be, too, Felicia. But our secret is to stay our secret."

She watched him finger the envelope as he stared out the window. He seemed to be searching for a way to explain himself.

"One other thing," he said. "This is business. Everyone must use their head. Do you know what I mean?"

She nodded, though she didn't understand. None of this was making much sense.

"But I don't want it to be unpleasant for Nicky," Antonelli went on. "I want you to be nice to him. I want you to make him fall in love with you, so he will be happy. It's better for you, also, if he loves you."

She struggled to keep her voice steady. "You have more faith in love than I do, Mr. Antonelli."

He dismissed that with a wave of his hand. "A beautiful woman can always make a man love her. I could fall in love with you myself. It is all in your attitude."

Vinny Antonelli had put her in a neat trap. But Felicia knew there was still one way out...if she could pull it off. "I understand what you want from me, Mr. Antonelli. And I'll try. But what if it doesn't work? Maybe after your nephew meets me, he won't want to marry me. What then?"

She held her breath, knowing this was her trump card— her single best chance of getting out of this mess without angering the mob.

"That won't happen. He *will* marry you. And as for the love, as long as I hear from him that you tried very hard, that you were very nice, then I will accept whatever happens. But if you don't do your best, there will be trouble."

Vinny let his last words hang. Felicia was so scared that her heart almost stopped. She closed her eyes and pictured her father. He had known what they were facing. He'd understood.

Vinny patted her arm to get her attention. "I know this is not the marriage every girl dreams of," he went on, "but there are compensations."

He handed over the envelope. Inside she found ten one-thousand dollar bills and a photograph. She turned it over and saw the name Nick Mondavi written on the back.

"Have some pictures taken of yourself and send them to my wife," Vinny said. "Here's a slip of paper with her address and phone number. Call her, find out what kind of boy Nicky is. She will tell you what to do to make him love you. Women know these things, I don't have to tell you that. Use the money to buy clothes and perfume, whatever you need."

As he talked, Felicia studied the photograph. Nick Mondavi had dark brown hair and hazel eyes. His features were clear and strong. His no-nonsense jaw looked determined. All in all, she would have to say he was a handsome, prosperous-looking man. If her mother had showed her this picture instead of the one of the fat doctor, she would not have been reluctant to agree to dinner.

But this wasn't her mother setting her up with the son of a friend. Vinny Antonelli was a gangster demanding that she marry his nephew. And in spite of Nick Mondavi's good looks, Felicia knew there was no way a photo could tell her what kind of man he was. For all she knew, he could be a bastard, a pervert or worse.

Vinny Antonelli patted her knee in a grandfatherly way. "I know you're the right girl because this bothers you. If you were too eager, I'd wonder. But don't worry, Nicky is a good boy. In the end, you'll want him with or without the money."

She shook her head. "I'll do what you want, Mr. Antonelli. I'll marry your nephew, and I'll try to make him believe I love him. But you might as well know the whole thing will be an act. I will never love him. Ever. How could I care for any man who would let this happen to an innocent woman?"

Antonelli took a cigar from his coat pocket. He snipped off the end and then lit it with a gold lighter. Felicia watched as the smoke curled from his lips, and he lowered the window a crack.

"Who said Nicky let this happen? You're assuming he has a choice in this. He doesn't. I had to convince him, just like I had to convince you."

"You blackmailed your own nephew?"

He smiled. "I used a different persuasion. Necessity. But that changes nothing. Like it or not, you're both in the same boat."

# 4

DURING THE FLIGHT across country, Nick Mondavi tried to work on cash-flow projections for his properties, but he couldn't keep his mind on the data. He'd stare at the screen of his laptop computer, his eyes would glaze over, his mind would do a loop and he'd find himself thinking about Felicia Mauro. Three times he pulled her picture from his inside coat pocket and studied her face. How could such a lovely woman be willing to marry him, sight unseen?

Nick had found the whole business sufficiently sleazy that he initially decided against getting involved. If he was facing a fight for his life with the government, then he'd go it alone and trust that justice would prevail. Yes, the subpoena had been served, exactly as Uncle Vinny had predicted. Yes, the FBI had carted off his books. And yes, they seemed determined to tie him to his uncle's illicit operations. But thanks to Uncle Vinny's warning, Nick had been prepared for the ordeal.

He'd discussed the matter at length with a battery of attorneys. They were convinced that his properties were safe from confiscation given the lack of evidence of any laundering conspiracy. The consensus was that the government could tie him up, but they couldn't nail him to a cross. So Nick had decided against selling everything and moving his capital offshore, as his uncle had advised. But the immigration thing was proving to be more problematical. The government hadn't acted yet, but he had to be prepared in case they did.

The immigration law specialist he consulted had advised him that marriage to an American citizen would not prevent him from being deported, but she also told him it wouldn't hurt his case, especially since his first wife had been an Italian national and that did not signal the sort of attitude he needed to project. There was a strong psychological element to these cases, the attorney told him, and having an American wife and American children would be a plus.

That wasn't reason to run off and get married, of course, but it had been enough to entice him to his aunt's house when she called to say the girl Vinny had found in San Francisco was lovely. He'd gone over to have a look at the photos and get the sales pitch, expecting to be unconvinced. But a funny thing happened—he fell for the woman he saw in the pictures.

Not that he was under any illusion that a photograph could tell the real story. Beauty wasn't skin deep, and he'd never been the kind of guy who could be blown away by a pretty face. Sure, he appreciated a lovely woman, but he appreciated intelligence, character and personality even more.

But even so, he became intrigued. And Aunt Maria was insistent that he check Felicia out. "Who knows, you might like her. It sounds like she's from a nice family. Go to California, Nicky, what can it hurt?"

Even before he'd had that visit from one of Uncle Vinny's lawyers, Nick was tempted to meet the woman, if only to satisfy his curiosity. But the news the lawyer brought him added a new sense of urgency.

"Your uncle has gotten confirmation from his informer that the immigration thing is coming down very soon," he'd said. "If you're married before you're served, it'll be better. I wouldn't waste any time."

When the pilot lowered the flaps in preparation for landing in San Francisco, Nick stowed his gear. Then he took a few more moments to study the photo of Felicia. It was incredible to think he might actually marry the woman.

Nick slipped the photo into his pocket, telling himself it probably wouldn't work. Despite his desperation, it was hard to imagine he'd go through with it. After all, how could he want any woman who'd have him under these circumstances? There had to be something wrong with her. Either that or she'd been bought, which was just as bad.

FELICIA SAT on the rose and beige antique needlepoint chair her maternal grandmother had left her. She was in the front room of her apartment on Filbert Street, just off Columbus, nervously twisting her pearls as she waited for Nick Mondavi.

It had been a horrible week. Her entire life she'd tried to please everyone—to be true to herself and yet give her parents or her teachers or her friends what they wanted and expected. But Vinny Antonelli had not left room for that sort of compromise. She either cooperated fully or faced the consequences.

Resigning herself to the inevitable, Felicia had dutifully called Vinny's wife in New York. To her surprise, the woman had been charming, and effusive about Nicky, insisting that he was a good and honest man. Felicia had felt her hopes rise again on the theory that if Nick was truly decent, he wouldn't go through with this. Then she recalled Vinny saying that he hadn't given his nephew a choice in the matter.

So, with a heavy heart, Felicia had listened to the aunt's advice, taking notes on Nicky's likes and dislikes. Even now, Pavarotti's "Amore" was playing in the background, not so much because she liked it—though she did—but because the aunt had told her, "Nicky likes opera and is a fan of Pavarotti." Felicia had dutifully bought every CD Pavarotti had recorded.

She'd also bought several new outfits so she'd "look sharp for Nicky." Today she had on a new taupe cashmere sweater and matching skirt that had cost just over seven hundred dollars. It was modest, yet showed her figure. That formulation seemed most appropriate for a man who "appreciated a good-looking woman, but didn't like them blatant."

There were hundreds of dollars' worth of roses spread around the apartment. It looked like a funeral home, in her opinion, but she hadn't bought them. They'd been delivered that morning. She assumed that Nicky had sent them because "he liked roses."

She got up and went to the bay window. Her apartment was on the second floor and looked down on Filbert Street. There was no sign of Nick Mondavi. She consulted her watch. His plane, if it was on schedule, would have landed an hour ago. That would have given him enough time to check into his hotel and grab a taxi to her place. He could be arriving at any minute.

Felicia thought of how difficult the past few days had been. Though her mother was oblivious, her father suffered right along with her. Felicia had played down the threat in discussing it with him, but he was no fool. He knew that once a person got in bed with the mob, her life changed forever. His own story was proof of that. Sins of the father.

She turned from the window, her eyes falling on the photo of Nick that Vinny had given her. It was in a silver frame on her sideboard. She went over and picked it up. Gazing at his face, she asked herself for the millionth time how she should act when they met. And she would have to act, that was clear, because her genuine feelings were anger and fear and frustration.

For a while, she'd decided that if the aunt had been right about Nicky liking women who were refined and modest, then she'd act overeager to turn him off. But there was little doubt word would get back to Vinny, and she couldn't risk his taking it out on her father. Nor could she act too reluctant, for the same reason.

Her best, her only hope would be if Nick asked why she was willing to marry him. True, she couldn't defy Vinny outright and tell Nick about the favor. But if she did as Vinny suggested and told Nick about the money she'd be paid, then maybe pride would force him to reject her. Yes, that was her best hope. That Nick Mondavi would have a lot of pride.

THE TAXI pulled up in front of a rather nondescript apartment building, and the driver told him this was the place. Nick paid the fare and got out. He'd stopped at a florist along the way and gotten a dozen red roses, mainly because his aunt had suggested it. "This isn't easy for a modern girl," she'd told him. "Do what you can to spare her feelings."

Nick rang the bell and waited. He'd been telling himself it was too much to expect love, or even genuine regard. It would be enough if they acted decent to each other. After all, this was a business proposition as much as anything, though he still didn't know how she had been induced to marry him. "Your uncle did not speak of this," Aunt Maria said when he'd asked. "All I know is that she is a good girl and has agreed to be your wife."

There was no answer to his ring, so he pushed the button again. After a brief pause, a woman's voice crackled over the intercom.

"Yes?"

"It's Nick Mondavi," he said.

"Come on up. Second floor, front apartment," she said without discernible emotion.

He felt a twinge of apprehension as the door buzzed and he entered the building. He glanced around, trying to take in the fact that this was the home of his soon-to-be wife—if things went according to plan.

There was a vaguely musty smell to the place, but it seemed clean. He went to the stairs and started up. The carpeting, he noted, was worn, but not shabby. The building was ordinary, not at all special. And he told himself that Felicia Mauro wouldn't be special either. If she was, she wouldn't be in this position. The picture his aunt gave him would undoubtedly prove to be more enticing than the woman herself. He already knew that, too.

The newel post at the top of the stairs was worn smooth by years of use. Nick let his hand glide over it, knowing hers must have touched it daily. He went to the door closest to the front of the building, dread welling inside him. He rapped on the door.

After a few seconds, it swung open.

Felicia Mauro stood before him, so lovely he was stunned. Frozen. Her slight frown of uncertainty turned into a smile as she glanced at the flowers, then at him.

"Hello," she said simply.

He took her in, pleased that her figure was every bit as appealing as her face. She was very beautiful. Taller than he'd expected. Her dark hair was parted in the middle and fell past her shoulders in soft waves.

"I'm Nick Mondavi," he said.

There was a flicker of anxiety in her eyes, but she smiled again. It was a little tentative, a little stiff, but it was a smile. Yet for some strange reason Nick had the feeling that she would have preferred to close the door in his face. Not that he blamed her. In spite of her beauty, he would just as soon turn around and leave.

"Come on in," she said.

He entered, turning to her as she shut the door. "Oh . . . these are for you," he said, handing her the roses.

"How nice. Thank you."

He noticed then that the apartment was full of flowers. "You like roses," he remarked, nodding to one huge bouquet on the hall table, and another that he could see in the front room.

Felicia glanced around with him. "Yes. You were very generous, Nick, but I think maybe you overdid it a little."

"I didn't send them," he said, seeing her misapprehension.

"You didn't?"

He shook his head. "No. Maybe it was my uncle."

Her expression darkened. "Oh."

There was an awkward moment. Felicia stared at the floor, her cheeks turning red. "I'll see if I can find one more vase," she said without looking at him. "Please make yourself at home."

Nick watched her go, admiring her figure, wondering how in the hell his uncle had pulled this off. Was he about to fall into an unexpected bit of good luck, or was there a catch in this somewhere?

FELICIA HURRIED into the kitchen, set the roses down by the sink, and took a deep breath. All week long she'd imagined what it would be like to come face to face with Nick Mondavi. She'd run every possible scenario through her mind—that is, all but one. In spite of his picture, she hadn't expected him to be so attractive. And it wasn't just that he was good-looking. He actually did seem pretty nice.

She tiptoed to the archway leading into the living room and peeked in. She could see him. He had gone to the love seat and sat looking around. He seemed out of place—as if he was too big for her furniture, too big for her apartment, too big for her life. Yes, that was the problem. He was too big, too New York, too Mafia, in all probability.

She shouldn't let herself forget that, no matter how he seemed.

Felicia started opening cupboards, scrounging around for a vase big enough. The best she could come up with was an old wine carafe. She filled it with water and began putting the roses in it, all the while reminding herself that Vinny Antonelli had been a handsome man for his age, very distinguished-looking. But that didn't change who and what he was. Appearances often lied. The fact was, in dealing with Nick, she wasn't just dealing with a man, but with a family and a way of life.

Picking up the carafe, she took a deep breath and headed for the living room, careful to keep a bland expression on her face. The next few minutes would probably be the most critical in her entire life. She had to stay on her toes.

Nick glanced up as she set the roses on the coffee table in front of him. She started to sit down in the needlepoint chair, then changed her mind and sat on the couch. Close to him, but not too close.

"Is that *Tosca*, or am I mistaken?" he asked.

"You aren't mistaken."

He shifted uneasily. Felicia looked at her hands, praying he'd make the first move. She wanted to take her cue from him.

"This is awkward, isn't it?" he said.

She pressed her lips into a tight smile. "Yes. Very."

"I'm sorry...I mean, I don't enjoy putting you through this," he explained.

"I've felt it's more your uncle than you." As soon as the words were out of her mouth, Felicia wondered if she'd been too candid. But Nick didn't seem disturbed.

"Yes, I suppose that's true," he said mildly. There was another extended silence. He cleared his throat. "So tell me about yourself. My aunt said you worked in your family's restaurant."

She nodded. "I make the pastries and desserts."

"Interesting."

"I love to cook."

"That's good."

"Yes, I guess it is."

She nervously fiddled with her hands until she caught herself. In a way, this was worse than her first date. Nick was as nervous as she was. Of course, the trick would be to use that to her advantage. But how? He seemed to be holding the cards. All she could do was keep up her end of the conversation and hope he'd give her some kind of out.

"What do you do, Nick? Your aunt said something about real estate."

"I'm a developer."

"Oh. That's interesting."

Felicia felt tiny beads of perspiration forming on her lip. The room seemed too hot and yet too cold. She had to suppress a shiver. This was pure agony.

Suddenly, Nick got up, took a few steps, then turned to face her. He looked dismayed. Anxious and dismayed. Her heart nearly stopped.

"Under the circumstances, it's silly to play games. Do you really want to do this, Felicia? Get married, I mean?"

She was completely at a loss. How in the name of God should she answer that? The truth wouldn't do. But how far should she accommodate him? How compliant should she be? Her father's life was riding on this.

"Yes, don't you?"

"I think the fact I flew clear across the country to meet you speaks for itself."

She blinked at the curtness of his response. "You're right. It does."

He thought for a moment, then his expression softened. He seemed to relax. That was good, in a way, but she wasn't exactly striving for harmony. What she wanted was to create contention without seeming to do so. But how on earth did you appear to try to valiantly win somebody's heart while at the same time ensuring that you failed?

"I guess I'm having trouble understanding you." He ran his hand through his hair. "You aren't what I expected."

Felicia's breath wedged in her throat. Maybe he was trying to politely say he didn't like her, that she wouldn't do. God, she couldn't be that lucky, could she? "I don't know what to say, except that I'm sorry. I guess."

"No, no, that's not what I mean. You just...don't seem like the kind of woman who'd be willing to marry me sight unseen." He sighed. "I know that's blunt, but this is a situation that calls for directness."

He returned to the love seat and sat down. He was closer to her than before. She could feel the heat of his body, smell the tang of his after-shave. She told herself it didn't matter that he was good-looking and sexy. No. It mattered, but it only made a bad situation worse.

"Just tell me this," he said. "Why are you so willing to marry me? You don't look like you'd have trouble finding a man. You can't be desperate."

Felicia squeezed her hands together so firmly her knuckles turned white. This was what she'd been waiting for—the big question. But should she tell him about the money now, or wait? She took a deep breath, making her decision.

"After talking to your aunt, I realized it would be a very good . . . opportunity," she said in a measured tone.

"Opportunity?"

She drew another long breath. "Well," she said, "I'm thirty-five and you're a . . ."

"Good catch?"

"Yes."

"That's it? That's really it?"

"Well . . ."

"You don't really expect me to believe you're desperate to find a man, do you?" he asked. "A woman as attractive as you? No, there's something else going on here."

She opened her mouth to speak, but no words came out. This was worse even than being with Vinny. Felicia got to her feet. She walked to the window, then turned to face him, knowing the moment had come.

"I'd rather just say it up front and get it off my chest. I'm being paid."

He looked away for a moment, then back at her. "By my uncle, obviously."

"Yes."

"I see."

"I don't see any point in lying," she added quickly. "You wouldn't believe me if I said I loved you, because that's not possible. I don't even know you."

The words had come out in a rush. Felicia watched him carefully, knowing his reaction was key.

"Money can be very persuasive," he said.

Again she colored. "It's not the only reason," she said half under her breath.

"Why else? Not because you're . . . thirty-five and single."

"That happens to be true."

"Maybe, but you're not desperate, Felicia, I don't care what you say. I just don't buy it."

"I don't know how you can judge me," she said as she began to pace. "Obviously, if I loved someone else, or I . . . felt I had prospects, I wouldn't even consider marrying you, but . . ."

"You don't, so why not give it a go with me? Especially if there's a profit to be made?" He laughed. "Well, maybe. But all I can say is my uncle must have offered you one hell of a lot of dough."

"He did." Felicia looked him straight in the eye, praying silently. "I hope that doesn't bother you. The fact that

I'm being paid, I mean." She was almost afraid to breathe, knowing everything was resting on his answer. But to her dismay Nick only shrugged.

"Who am I to judge?"

She gulped. "Then you're satisfied?"

"I think I am now that we understand each other."

The wind went right out of her. She sensed that as far as Nick was concerned, it was a done deal. This whole time, she'd been tilting at windmills. All Nick wanted to do was confirm that she wasn't a tramp or something.

A part of her died right then and there. She felt empty. Lost. Maybe she'd known all along that there would be no way out of this, but she'd had to try. Tears welled in her eyes, and she turned away so that he wouldn't see.

"Don't you feel the same?" he asked, apparently sensing something was wrong.

"Oh, yes," she said, smiling and blinking away her tears. "I'm really pleased." She wiped her eyes. "It's an emotional subject."

"I suppose it is."

Felicia drew a ragged breath. "Well, since that's settled," she began, with more assurance than she truly felt, "do you feel like telling me what the big rush is for? I know you have to get married quickly, but I don't know why."

"Because I don't have much choice. I'm surprised my uncle didn't tell you. The simple fact is, the government may try to deport me."

"Why?"

As he told the story, Felicia was struck by the irony of the situation. Because of a favor her father owed to Vinny Antonelli—and because Vinny had brought Nick to the States illegally—she and Nick Mondavi were going to marry. It seemed absurd that actions taken decades earlier should now lead to two innocent people's lives being changed forever. Of course, Nick wasn't really innocent. Not in the sense she was. He, at least, had a choice.

When he finished, she turned to him. "I still don't know why you didn't just find someone on your own. Your aunt said you were a catch. So why aren't women flocking to your door? Why do you need me?" She regarded him, taking in his strong jaw, aware of the light in his eyes. Looking at him like that made her feel warm. "I don't see any obvious flaws."

He chuckled. "Thanks."

"It was a serious comment."

"Actually, I was married once, Felicia. Happily married. But my wife died."

"Oh." In spite of everything, she felt a rush of sympathy for him. "I'm sorry. No one told me."

"Don't apologize. Enough time's passed that I could have found someone else, if it had been a priority. But it hasn't."

"I see."

"So the bottom line is I need a wife. And the sooner the better. Does that change things for you?" he asked.

She shook her head, wishing she could blurt out the truth but not daring to give him so much as a hint. "There's no reason it should."

"Don't reply too hastily," he said. He suddenly looked uncomfortable again. "You do understand, don't you, that this can't have the appearance of a sham marriage? To the Feds, this is more than just another immigration case."

She slowly nodded. "You mean because of your uncle?"

"That's right."

She shifted uneasily, aware that they were getting down to the fundamental issue of what this marriage would mean to each of them.

"I know the question seems absurd, considering you just agreed to marry me, but how far are you willing to go?" he asked. "Are you prepared to be more than a wife in name only?"

Her heart was pounding. She swallowed hard. "You're asking if I'll agree to have sex with you."

"In effect, yes. My lawyers tell me the Immigration and Naturalization Service can ask very pointed questions. You don't have to actually fall in love with me, of course, but you'll have to act like you have." Nick took her hand and looked right into her eyes. "There's no point in kidding ourselves. If we can't agree on this up front, there'll be trouble down the road."

Felicia could feel the energy flowing from his hand to hers. He seemed warm. Very warm. "I'll do what I have to do."

"So will I."

"Then I guess we're agreed," she said, feeling the need to confirm her worst fears.

"I guess we are."

Nick gave her hand a squeeze, but her heart was aching so badly she hardly noticed.

"I'm glad to see you didn't agonize over it," he said.

Felicia pulled her hand away, telling herself to buck up. At least the uncertainty was over. There would be no getting out of this. But she still didn't understand Nick. He seemed decent enough on the surface. Yet he hadn't hesitated to agree to take her as his wife, even knowing she was doing it for money. What did that say about him?

In a way, of course, it didn't matter. No. It mattered, but it didn't change things. That was the right formulation. She looked at him, trying to decide what kind of man she'd agreed to marry. He returned her gaze, his eyes shifting to her mouth, then her breasts. It wasn't hard to guess what he was thinking.

"Do you mind if I ask what your limits are?" he said. "Or is your deal with my uncle that anything goes?"

Felicia blanched. "I agreed to be whatever kind of wife you needed."

"What do you mean by 'whatever'?"

She didn't like the question. Did he take some sort of perverse pleasure in rubbing her nose in it? Well, if that's what he wanted, she'd give it to him. "Tell me to laugh, Nick," she said stiffly, "and I'll laugh. Tell me to cry and I'll cry. If you want the INS to think I love you, I'll make them think I do. If you want me to get . . . pregnant, I'll do that, too. I'm completely at your disposal."

He blinked.

"That's why your uncle is paying me. Surely you aren't surprised."

Nick quickly recovered. There was a gleam in his eye, but it only lasted a moment. Then his eyes narrowed and his expression turned judgmental. If she didn't know better, she'd have thought he was disgusted.

She sat up a bit straighter, trying to be as dignified as possible. It hurt, knowing that he probably regarded her as no better than a streetwalker. But the worst part was that he hadn't been too disgusted to take advantage of the situation—just disgusted enough to look down on her because of it.

"What's the matter?" she said. "Isn't this what you expected?"

"Hearing a beautiful woman say something like what you just said is every man's fantasy."

"So?"

"So why am I not elated?"

"I don't know."

He stared at her breasts blatantly then.

"Are you upset?" she asked.

"No."

"I'm trying to be accommodating," she said, obviously not believing him.

"It's the immigration service you have to fool, Felicia, not me. But I don't know why we're discussing this. We've agreed to marry. We only have to be concerned about the practical problems at this point." He cleared his throat

again. "I'm told the quickest and easiest way is to go to
Nevada. Can you do whatever you have to do in two or
three days?"

She took a breath, fighting a sinking feeling. "I think
so."

"My aunt told me your family is close. How will your
parents feel about a sudden marriage?"

"My father will understand. My mother may in time."

"They don't know about...your arrangement with my
uncle?"

She hesitated. "No."

"They think their beautiful daughter would only marry
for love."

Felicia felt the pain of regret. For herself, for her parents
and especially for her father.

"Listen," he said before she could respond, "we're getting married for my convenience, but I don't see any reason to hurt your parents' feelings. Ask them to the
wedding, if you want. Do whatever you think's necessary."

He seemed to be pulling back slightly. Probably realizing he'd been rather insensitive. "Thanks," she said, "but
it would probably cause more harm than good. My
mother wouldn't understand a loveless wedding."

"If you can put on an act for me, Felicia, I can give you
a couple of days of loving fiancé in return. You may not
need it, but your parents might. Or am I wrong?"

"You're willing to pretend?"

"Sure, why not? I'm not completely heartless."

"I know my mother would be grateful. I've been worrying how I'd explain this."

"Sometimes honesty's not the way to go."

She nodded solemnly. "Yes, you're right. Unfortunately."

He got up. "We'll need a story. How about I've been
coming out here on business for months...we've been

seeing each other . . . and this trip I popped the question? Would they buy that?"

"My social life has been an issue in the family," she said. "My mother wouldn't be surprised that I hid something like this so as not to raise expectations. I could say I waited till I was sure you were serious." Consternation filled her face. "Are you sure you want to do this?"

He shrugged. "Consider it a wedding gift. Your parents' happiness." He reached in his pocket, took out a diamond ring and handed it to her. "This makes it official."

Felicia held the ring. It was a two-carat diamond.

"Put it on," he said. "We might as well start practicing."

She slid the ring on her finger and contemplated it. Then she looked at him. She didn't speak.

"Does it fit?"

She nodded, hating the coldness with which he was doing this, though there was no reason to expect anything else. She fought back her emotion.

"What's next?" he asked. "Do I have to ask your father for your hand? Are they old-fashioned that way?"

She shook her head. A tear ran down her cheek.

"What's the matter?" he asked.

"My mother will be very happy," she said. "Thank you."

"Oh." He shifted uneasily. "When do I meet your parents?"

"I'll ask them over for dinner tonight, if that's okay."

"Fine."

She stood. The smile she gave him was genuine for the first time. "I don't know why, but I feel better about this. I guess because you're being so nice about my parents. Thanks."

"I'm not all bad." He offered his hand. "I hope being married to me won't be too unpleasant."

She looked brave through her tears. "That depends on you a lot more than it depends on me." She slipped her slender fingers in his, her eyes glistening. "Just don't resent me," she said. "That's all I ask."

"Resent you? For saving my butt?"

"Men sometimes blame women for their disappointments." She glanced at her ring. "I think it's safe to say neither of us would have made this our first choice."

"That goes without saying."

Felicia bit her lip. She looked into his eyes, nodding. "Yes," she said, her voice scarcely above a whisper, "I guess it does."

# 5

CARLO MAURO turned the stem of his wineglass, shaking his head. "What good does it do that he's considerate if he takes the life of my only child?"

"Pops," she said, taking his hand, "think how much worse it could be. We should be glad he thinks of my family."

"So am I to thank him? Is that what you want?"

His voice had gone up with the last words, and Felicia glanced across the nearly empty restaurant. One of the chefs was having a cup of coffee with a neighborhood man before the dinner shift began. They were preoccupied and didn't hear.

"Felicia," Carlo went on, lowering his voice, "to be honest, I'd rather never see this man. I might kill him."

"I know, Papa. But it's Mama I'm thinking of. Why should she suffer? It's bad enough knowing your heart is aching."

He reached out and touched her cheek, his eyes shimmering. "I can't begin to tell you what this is doing to me, knowing it is all my fault."

"It doesn't do any good to beat yourself. You were only a boy when you got into that fight. You couldn't have known what would happen."

"It would have been better if Joey killed me, instead of me killing him," Carlo said, taking out his handkerchief and wiping his eyes. "Ten thousand nights I prayed for his soul, and now God takes his revenge on my beautiful child."

"Nick could be a lot worse, believe me."

"Maybe. But you must never forget who his people are," Carlo said, wagging his finger. "The devil could smile, too."

"Pops, are you trying to make me feel better or worse?"

Carlo took her hands as tears streamed down his face. "I've been thinking. Maybe we should leave town. The three of us could go to Rio."

"No, Papa. There's your health to consider. And Mama would die if she had to leave her home. Besides, they'd find us. You know they would. This way, Mama will have her illusions."

Carlo wiped his eyes and blew his nose. "You don't know how hard it will be to come tonight and drink to his happiness."

"Then just come for dessert. You'll only have to stay an hour that way."

Carlo drew a fortifying breath. "All right. I will do whatever you and your mother wish."

"Then I'd better go talk to her. It will take her a while to recover when I tell her I'm getting married in two days."

"Do you want me to go with you?"

"No, it's best if I do it myself." She checked her watch. "There's not much time. I still have to cook dinner." Felicia slipped from the booth. Before leaving the table she kissed her father's bald head. "I'm trying hard to pretend that marrying Nick is what I want, Pops. You should do the same."

Carlo Mauro nodded. But he was too emotional to speak. Felicia pinched his cheek and headed for the door. She said goodbye to the men as she passed by.

"You're looking beautiful as always, Felicia," one of them said. "No wonder your father is so proud."

She smiled in reply. Then, pushing the door open, she glanced at her father. He was draining the wine from his glass, immersed in his misery. Felicia knew this was as hard on him as it was on her. Maybe more so.

BY THE TIME she left her parents' house on Telegraph Hill the evening fog had rolled in and San Francisco was wearing its usual shroud of gray. Felicia hurried along, the collar of her coat turned up, knowing she would be pressed to have everything ready when Nick arrived.

In her hands was a shallow baking dish filled with some of her mother's freshly made lemon-garlic linguini. "I made this for your father's dinner, but you won't have time to make fresh pasta, so serve it to your Nick with my blessing," Louisa Mauro had said. "All I ask is that you give me credit. A boy should know his mother-in-law can cook."

Her mother had taken the news better than expected, but there was a long moment of silence following the announcement. Louisa had sat very still, her hands gripping the arms of the chair as she searched Felicia's eyes. Then she'd said in a tremulous voice, "Are you pregnant?"

"No, Mama, I'm not pregnant," she'd replied with a laugh.

Her mother had let out a sigh of relief. "Thank God."

They'd embraced, and Louisa shed the obligatory tears. Then she pulled back.

"So, why the sudden wedding? Why not wait and do it right?"

"Mama, Nick wants to get married right away, and I told him I'd elope, but only if you and Papa can come to the ceremony... if you want to, that is."

"How could I not? I've only been waiting thirty-five years for this. But what priest will marry you on two days' notice?"

"Mama, I don't think it will be a church wedding."

"You said this Nick is a good Catholic boy, didn't you? Of course he will marry you in the church."

"I'm sure he'd like to, but there's just not time. Besides this is his second wedding."

"But he's not divorced. His wife died, you said. Isn't it true?"

"Yes, Mama. But please don't make an issue. It will only cause problems."

Her mother had fallen silent, obviously weighing the joy of marriage against the disappointment of a civil ceremony. Felicia had done her best to distract her.

"Would you really have been upset if I said I was pregnant?" Felicia had asked.

"Of course. I know it happens all the time these days, but not to the best girls."

"Well, you can sleep easy tonight, Mama. The family still has its honor. I'm definitely not pregnant."

"Good. But if you want my advice, you'll start trying to have a baby on your wedding night. You're not a girl anymore. And you don't want to be forty before you've had your second."

"First things first, Mama," she'd said with a laugh, and they'd hugged again.

Felicia had put on a brave front, but her heart was aching. Everything she'd said was a lie, pure artifice for the sake of her mother's happiness. It was worse even than if she'd married the fat doctor to make her parents happy. At least the doctor was what he was represented to be. Nick Mondavi was a fraud.

When she reached Lombard Street at the foot of Telegraph Hill, a taxi happened along. She flagged it down. Her place was only eight blocks away, but a cab would save fifteen minutes. An hour and a half was not a lot of time to whip up a gourmet meal and get ready, too.

The mousse was setting in the fridge and she had the Greek olives, roasted portobello mushrooms, provolone and Italian salami on hand for antipasto. Most of her time would be taken up washing the romaine for the Caesar salad, and making the garlic-cream wine sauce for the pasta. Cleaning the shrimp would only take a few minutes. The crab meat and the scallops required no work. As her mother was fond of saying, "Fast food doesn't have to come frozen in a box."

Felicia had told her mother that she'd never cooked for Nick before, but it was about the only thing she'd said that was true. "The first dinner is the one they always remember," Louisa said. "It must be perfect." That was what had prompted the offer of the fresh lemon-garlic linguini.

As the taxi passed their restaurant on Washington Square, Felicia thought of her poor father, the way he was suffering. In a way, that was what she'd hated most—seeing him helpless and guilt-ridden. Vinny Antonelli was to blame. But so was Nick. The situation might not have been his fault, but he didn't have to destroy her life to save his own. He could have said no to his uncle. He could have walked away.

FELICIA WAS PUTTING on the pearl stud earrings she'd bought at Gumps with money her parents had given her for her thirtieth birthday when the intercom buzzed. She jumped—which was no surprise since she'd gotten progressively more nervous as seven o'clock approached. Before letting Nick in, she stepped back for a look in the mirror. She was in a scoop-neck long sleeve black dress made of fine wool. She'd gotten it Saturday with Vincent Antonelli's money, along with a pair of matching black pumps.

Before she started for the entry to let Nick in, she put on the diamond ring he'd given her. She'd taken it off right after he left and then forgot about it. Of course, if this had been a real engagement, she'd never have taken it off. But she was sure that he couldn't care less whether she even liked the damn thing. He'd probably gotten it more for the benefit of the Immigration and Naturalization Service than for her.

She went to the intercom. "Yes?"

"It's me, Nick."

She buzzed him in and went to the kitchen for a quick look at the sauce. It was on low and fortunately showed no signs of thickening. She stirred it, then went to the door, arriving just as he knocked.

Nick wore a black double-breasted Italian suit with a white shirt and dark red silk tie. His hair was slicked down and seemed darker than in his picture. It was that suave New York look—which normally she didn't care for—but on him, she had to admit, it was appealing. Very appealing.

Nick was checking her out at the same time she examined him.

"Don't you look nice," he said, smiling with an expression of sincerity that was, at best, ambiguous.

A strange awareness came over her. This was the man, she reminded herself, she was to marry in a matter of a few days. A total stranger. "You, too, Nick."

She hadn't noticed the bottle of wine in his hand until he extended it to her. "I meant to bring more red roses," he said with a wry grin, "but there don't seem to be any left in town."

She smiled dutifully. "No, they're all here."

She motioned for him to enter. Nick sauntered into the room, glancing around. "No parents?"

She closed the door. "They're coming for dessert. It'll be the two of us for dinner."

"Oh. It's just as well," he said. "I wasn't looking forward to a lot of dinner table conversation about our plans."

"No, I imagine you weren't."

He was looking at her again, and it wasn't innocently. She couldn't say his expression was salacious, but he was seeing her as a woman, not as a business partner. Maybe he was imagining her as a wife. Or in bed.

"So, how did things go with your parents?" he asked.

"As well as could be expected. My mother was so pleased at the thought of me marrying that she didn't object too much to the negatives."

"The negatives?"

"The rush . . . the fact that they hadn't even met you."

Nick shrugged as though it couldn't be helped. But then, it wasn't his problem. She did have to give him credit for being considerate of their feelings, though. She owed him that.

Felicia studied the label on the wine. "Italian."

"A favorite of mine. I have cousins in Italy who send me a case every year. I was surprised to find it in San Francisco."

"We're not as provincial as you New Yorkers like to think."

He poked his tongue in his cheek. "I hope this marriage isn't going to be tainted by chauvinistic rivalry, the old east coast, west coast thing."

"I think that's the least of our worries, don't you, Nick?" She gestured for him to sit. "Make yourself comfortable. I'll check my sauce and then open this."

She headed for the kitchen, glad for the respite. At a superficial level, this could have been a first date. Not that she cooked for men all that often. She didn't. In fact, it had been months since she'd so much as gone to a movie with anyone. But that was only part of the reason she was nervous. This man was to become her husband, and she didn't even know him!

Felicia was at the stove, stirring her sauce, when he said, "How'd your mother like your ring?"

She jumped, not knowing he'd followed her to the kitchen. "Oh," she said, turning to face him. "You scared me."

Nick was again looking at her body, her clingy knit dress.

"To be honest, I forgot to take it. And she didn't ask. I think she was too much in shock to even think about it."

Nick contemplated her. He probably hadn't heard what she'd said. He definitely was thinking of her sexually. She could see it in his eyes. It made her feel nervous, trapped even.

When he started toward her, she stiffened, her breath catching because she didn't know what to do. But he reached past her, taking the bottle of wine from the counter next to her.

"Where's your corkscrew?" he asked. "I'll open this."

Felicia made an audible sigh of relief. "Oh. It's in the second drawer down," she said, pointing.

As Nick moved by her, she could smell his cologne again. She'd always been aware of the way men smelled, maybe because aromas were important to her. Food, people, places, all had signature odors—identifying, unique scents. Nick's was curiously enticing.

Felicia glanced over at him as he uncorked the bottle.

"Ashamed, were you?" he said.

"Pardon?"

"The reason you didn't take the ring."

"Oh."

When she didn't say more, he said, "Well?"

"What should I be ashamed of?" she asked. "The ring, or marrying you?"

Nick grinned. "Take your pick."

"Ashamed isn't a word I'd choose."

He removed the cork from the bottle. "Glasses?"

Felicia put down the spoon and, moving past him, took some wineglasses from the cupboard next to him. She felt his eyes on her. There was a look of bemusement on his face when she turned to him.

Nick touched her hands as he took the two glasses from her. "What word would you choose, Felicia?"

She took half a step back, not so much because of what he said, but the way he was saying it. Nick was definitely playing the man-woman thing. He was being seductive. She wanted to ask him what the hell for. Why was he doing this? To have fun?

"Uncomfortable," she said. "This whole thing makes me feel very uncomfortable."

"Are we talking about having to deal with your parents, going through a wedding ceremony or marriage to me?"

"All of the above."

He thought for a moment, then said, "I guess you agreed to do it, not like it."

There was cynicism and annoyance in his tone. Suddenly Felicia was afraid that maybe she'd been a little too candid. After all, Vincent Antonelli had asked—no, *ordered* her to satisfy Nick. Marrying him was only the beginning of what was expected of her.

Nick poured some wine into each of the glasses and handed her one. "How about if we drink to comfort?" he said. "That seems safe enough, don't you think?"

"I hope you weren't offended by what I said."

"Why should I be? People get paid for their work. That doesn't necessarily mean they have to enjoy it."

He was being snide. Felicia started to respond in kind, then thought better of it. After all, he could think what he wanted. She was doing what his uncle had forced her to do—nothing more. The unfortunate part was Nick was oblivious. She would have liked him to know the truth, understand the suffering he and his relatives were causing.

"To comfort, then," she said.

Nick touched his glass to hers and they drank. When he looked into her eyes the snideness was gone. Bemusement had replaced it. One brow rose slightly, flirtatiously. Felicia wanted to ignore it, but she couldn't. Nick Mondavi had a charm that affected her despite her feelings. She could see he was going to milk this for what he could.

She stirred the cream sauce once more before they went to the front room. She went to the love seat and Nick chose to sit beside her, slipping his arm easily behind her.

Felicia felt tense and tried not to let it show, though Nick must have noticed how stiff she was. She turned the stem of her wineglass and avoided looking at him.

After a while Nick touched the soft curls at her neck. It was a casual gesture, but it made her tremble.

"So, tell me why you aren't married and have a couple of little monsters hanging on your apron," he said.

"I don't know," she said, swallowing. "It just hasn't happened."

"You mean the right guy never came along?"

Her stomach tightened and she shifted uncomfortably. The question wasn't inappropriate or impolite, but she didn't like talking about Johnny. Especially not to strangers. "That's as good a way to put it as any," she said.

"Men in California must be shy. It's hard to believe someone like you could go unattached for long."

It seemed a compliment. She decided it was. "Thank you."

"I'm sincere," he said, letting his finger brush her neck.

Felicia jumped up instinctively. She looked at the table. "Why don't we eat now?" she blurted. "I'll get the antipasto. You can go to the table."

She handed him her wineglass, nearly dropping it in the process, then hurried off. When she got to the kitchen, her cheeks were burning, her breath coming in unsteady gasps. What was the matter with her? All he'd done was touch her.

For several moments she leaned against the counter. She couldn't remember feeling this way before—not since

Johnny. Maybe that was it. Nick's questions made her think of Johnny, the humiliation. What she was going through now was humiliating, too. That might account for it.

It took a few seconds to gather herself. She told herself she'd better get used to him. In a few days she'd be his wife.

Felicia took the plate of antipasto and carried it to the table in the dining room. Nick was standing at her chair, ready to help seat her. Then he went to his place at the other end of the table. She told him to help himself, avoiding his eyes. He took some grilled portobello mushrooms, olives and salami, then handed her the plate.

"So, have there been any close calls?" he asked.

She gave an anxious sigh. "You're determined, aren't you?"

"A man should know his wife, don't you think?"

There would be no skirting the issue. "All right, Nick, I'll tell you. I was engaged at twenty," she said, taking a mushroom. "My parents planned the biggest wedding North Beach had seen in a decade. We went to the church. All my friends and relatives were there. We waited and waited. Johnny never showed up. I was jilted, Nick, left at the altar. Does that satisfy you?"

"That was a long time ago."

"There hasn't been anyone since."

"Do you know why he disappeared?"

"Oh, I heard, eventually. Johnny was a stockbroker with a good firm on Montgomery Street, but he had a gambling problem I knew nothing about. He was into the bookies up to his eyeballs, according to his friends. Over a hundred thousand in the hole when he took off, was what I heard. To dump the debt he had to dump me—or at least he thought he did. Supposedly they were going to cut off a finger or something the day of our wedding if he didn't come up with twenty-five grand. I understood his fear but I thought he at least owed me a phone call. I guess he didn't see it that way, though."

"That's rough."

"It wasn't a confidence-builder."

"So, one jerk ruined your life."

"I don't know if I would put it that way," she said. "There hasn't been anyone else I've cared for, that's all."

"You must have loved him a lot."

She didn't like his probing but told herself not to let it get to her. Nick obviously thought she'd conceded certain rights when she'd agreed to marry him. "Johnny probably didn't deserve it, but I loved him. I'd have done anything for him—including running off with him to Mexico, South America or wherever he went."

"But he didn't ask."

"No."

"Ever hear from him again?" he asked, popping a roasted mushroom into his mouth.

"No."

Nick chewed, watching her. Felicia felt the color rising in her cheeks. He wasn't gloating. He wasn't amused. Whether he thought less of her because of it, she couldn't tell, but he was definitely deciding what her past said about her. He sipped his wine, but he didn't say anything more.

She unconsciously drummed her fingers on the table until she couldn't hold her tongue any longer. "Does that make me unworthy in your eyes?"

Nick considered that. "No, but I think I understand you better."

She wasn't sure what he meant. That he now understood why she'd reached thirty-five and hadn't married? Or that why, having no prospects, she'd agree to marry someone for money?

"Are you disappointed?" she asked.

"No. Do you wish I were?"

"Why would I do that?"

Nick stared at his wine contemplatively, then looked up and smiled. "A part of me thinks you'd like me to get up and walk out of here, never to be seen again."

"Like Johnny, you mean?"

"For different reasons, obviously."

Felicia got up. "I have to toss the salad and put the pasta on."

She went around the table to get his plate. Nick reached out and took her hand, holding it as she stood there. She caught his distinctive scent again. Her heart beat faster, and her knees began to shake.

"I'm not trying to give you a hard time," he said, rubbing the back of her hand with his thumb. "I just want to know who you are."

"I'm not your typical single woman," she said.

"I already figured that out."

"Maybe I'm damaged goods. Maybe I should admit that up front."

"While I can still change my mind?" He said it with a smile.

"You have that option."

"Your Johnny hurt you a lot, didn't he?"

"More than I should have allowed."

"I want to know what you meant when you said you're damaged goods."

She sighed. "I was practically catatonic after he left. It was all I could do to eat, dress and go to work. I tried to have a social life after a while, but it just didn't work. I was dead inside. If I went on a date it was for my mother's sake. When a man kissed me, I felt nothing." She looked into his eyes. "Does that answer your question?"

"It's a tragic story," he said, gazing at her.

"Yes, it is." Felicia removed her hand from his, took his plate and went to the kitchen. Her eyes were shimmering, and she was on the point of tears. She took a tissue and wiped her eyes carefully. Why she'd allowed herself to become so emotional she didn't know. She was confused. That was all she could say for sure.

It had to be obvious to Nick that her heart wasn't in this marriage, even as a business proposition. But she couldn't come right out and tell him why. She couldn't even be honest about her suffering. She'd lost control of her life. Maybe that was what bothered her most of all.

NICK LISTENED to the sounds she made in the kitchen. For some reason he imagined she was angry, or at least upset. This was not playing out as he'd expected. Felicia was either very strange or very clever. He hadn't decided which. For a woman who'd essentially prostituted herself, she was certainly doing a lot of negative selling. His uncle hadn't paid her yet, he knew that. Vincent Antonelli was shrewd and would never pay until he got everything he wanted from someone. Uncle Vinny knew how to use people, how to keep them in line, how to get them to do his bidding. In Felicia, he had a strange accomplice.

Which was why Nick decided she was more clever than eccentric. She was making him work at this, playing on his sympathies and emotions. After all, a woman who was bought and paid for didn't have many ways to play hard-to-get. And yet, it didn't seem like an act. Not completely.

It could be that she was one of those women who knew how to let the truth work for her regardless of the objective. You have a hard luck story, tell it. You have trouble with men, let a guy know it. Every man who ever lived wanted to succeed where other guys had failed. It could be as simple as that.

Felicia returned with the salad. She held the bowl while he put some on his plate. He was aware of her heady feminine scent. For a woman who claimed to have been ready for the nunnery, she had a strong, unmistakable sexuality. He didn't doubt her story, though. It had the ring of truth. But he didn't quite buy her innocence.

Nick hadn't exactly been in a social whirl since Gina had died. To the contrary, he'd kept his relationships superficial, the sex as impersonal as he could make it. Maybe that was why this woman with her contradictions and mixed signals intrigued him so. Maybe it was just the accident of chemistry.

"Go ahead and eat your salad," she said, after putting a few lettuce leaves on her plate and heading to the kitchen. "I'm having trouble getting my sauce to thicken properly."

"Even the experts struggle," he called after her.

"You don't ever struggle at your work?" she asked from the kitchen.

"All the time," he replied. "In development, ten failures are necessary for every success."

"If you were a chef, you'd have to kill yourself with a record like that, Nick."

He smiled. "That's why everybody's different. It would be pretty boring if we were all the same, don't you think?"

There was no response. He wasn't sure she'd heard him. He thought about their exchange, wondering if it had flowed naturally from the circumstances or if Felicia was playing him. It could be that she was a lot more adept with men than she was letting on. She might even have gotten a few tips from his aunt. "Nicky likes sweet, innocent girls." Nick could almost hear Aunt Maria saying something like that.

He finished his salad and moments later she was back, placing a plate of linguini before him. Chunks of crab, scampi and scallops were nestled in the creamy sauce. Sprinkled over it was fresh parmigiano reggiano.

"Wow," he said, admiringly, "you're the whole package, aren't you?"

"I cook."

"You're also modest."

She took her seat. Nick waited for her to pick up her fork.

"Don't suppose you cooked for my uncle."

"No, I didn't."

The harshness in her tone told him he'd ventured into dangerous waters. The fleeting dark look on her face confirmed it. Uncle Vinny evidently reminded her of the more unpleasant aspects of the venture. No surprise in that. He'd been the one who'd bought her, after all. If there was a silver lining in this, it was that Felicia didn't feel comfortable with what she'd done . . . unless, of course, that, too, was part of her act.

Nick took a bite of linguini. It was delicious. "This is wonderful," he said, hoping to guide things to safer waters.

"Thank you. The pasta my mother made. She said I should be sure to give her credit."

"You're a good daughter, I can tell."

"My mother assumes I love you. And she thinks you will be her son-in-law because you love me, so she cares what you think." She paused. "I'm sorry, but I couldn't tell her otherwise."

He studied her face, the soft auburn waves framing her pale skin. Felicia neither looked nor sounded like what she was. The picture of her, he now realized, was nothing compared to the real thing. He felt himself falling for her. Or perhaps, more accurately, for her act. This was a masterful performance. When a victim could watch himself being devoured and enjoy it, too, the predator definitely had skill.

"I want your mom to be happy," he said.

"If you want to please her, mention the pasta when they come."

"Thank you, I will."

They ate in silence, but he watched her. Felicia, wounded or not, was a fox—unorthodox, perhaps, but enticing as any woman he'd ever known. She took a bite of pasta, first spinning the linguini on the fork, then sliding it off the fork with her lips. There was something extra sensual about the way she ate. Maybe it came from being around food her whole life.

She speared a chunk of crab with her fork. "Is it true you went to Harvard?" she asked him.

"Yes."

"Did your uncle arrange that, too?"

There was bite in her tone. "Was that sarcasm I heard?"

"It was a serious question."

"No, he didn't arrange it," he said pointedly. "If he'd tried I probably wouldn't have gotten in."

"Really."

"You've branded me with my uncle's sins, Felicia. At least that's the way it's beginning to sound."

"I try not to make judgments."

"Oh, really? Seems to me everybody does."

"I'm sorry, then. Maybe I do think of you and your uncle as the same."

"We're not."

"Okay. If you say so."

Nick watched her eat. Felicia wouldn't look at him. She made a point of not looking at him. She was cool and compliant, aloof yet deferential, biting and submissive and defiant...all at the same time. She was trying to make him crazy, that's what she was doing. Gina had taught him that about women—they knew how to tell you no in saying yes. Yes with their lips, no with their eyes. There could be one thing in their minds, another in their hearts.

"Tell me something, Felicia. Are you hating this as much as you seem to be?"

She looked up with alarm. There was horror in her eyes. "No, Nick."

"Are you sure?"

She put down her fork. "Yes. I'm mean, if I gave you that impression . . . I'm sorry. Really."

Her concern seemed genuine. Then Nick understood. He saw the invisible hand of his uncle. She didn't want him complaining to Vinny. It was the mind-heart thing. Internal conflict. Her mind was saying, "I desperately want to marry you . . . for the money." Her heart was saying, "Oh, God, I don't even know this guy."

Nick was sort of in the same boat, except that he was intrigued by Felicia Mauro. That complicated things, but it also made them more interesting. He did have mixed feelings. It was like when he was at Harvard and his uncle had sent him a car, a two-year-old Porsche 911. On the one hand, he liked the car, on the other he didn't want it handed to him. There was something to be said for earning what you got.

"So, tell me," he said, "is there anything special I should know about your parents before they get here?"

She seemed relieved at the change of subject. "My father may be withdrawn. It's best to let him be. My mother will appreciate your attention."

"I'll remember to compliment her on the linguini."

That brought a smile. It was very clear that family was important to her. That was the only thing about Felicia he'd found so far that wasn't ambiguous.

"There is one thing," she said, hesitating.

"What's that?"

"My mother's very devout. She doesn't like it that we're not going to be married by a priest. I'm telling you so you'll know in case she brings it up. I've tried to explain that this is . . . an unusual marriage."

"You haven't told her why we . . ."

"No. I saw no point."

She shifted uneasily, and Nick could see it was a sensitive issue. She didn't want her mother to know that she was . . . well, a woman who could be bought. "I'll be sensitive to the issue," he said.

"Thank you. I won't ask for much, but to the extent my parents can be spared, I am grateful."

"That will be my gift to you, Felicia."

She smiled, looking pleased. "Then I will be a happy wife."

They finished eating, and she got up to clear the table. As she leaned over to take his plate he had a strong desire to touch her. He restrained himself, but he couldn't help but savor the notion of having her, even as he felt guilty about it.

It was the Porsche all over again. That sleek sports car had looked beautiful, as well. The parallel wasn't surprising. Felicia's compliance had been a gift, just like the car.

# 6

FELICIA WAS shaving chocolate onto the whipped cream that crowned the goblets of mousse as she listened to her mother in the dining room. Louisa either adored Nick or she was putting on a terrific act. And Nick, to his credit, was doing a credible job of playing the loving fiancé.

She'd been stunned at his deftness with her mother's first broadside of the evening. After their arrival, her father had taken their coats to the bedroom as Louisa took Nick's arm, leading him to the love seat.

"Why do you have to marry so quickly?" she asked. "What harm to wait a while so we can give you a wedding to be proud of?"

"If you knew how much I love Felicia," he replied, "you'd understand. From knowing Felicia, I know how she was raised—the kind of family she comes from. I want her with me as soon as possible. And out of respect to you and Mr. Mauro and Felicia, I wanted to marry her before taking her away."

It was a bald-faced lie, but he hadn't choked on his words. His salvation was in the fact that he'd done it for her and her mother, not himself. It was a kindness, albeit the most ironic sort.

Felicia had been more worried about her father than her mother, but Carlo had kept his cool. He was mostly silent, though he did manage to speak when propriety required it.

The lull in the conversation in the front room was followed by her mother's appearance in the kitchen.

"He's a wonderful man, honey. The perfect son-in-law."

"I'm glad you like him, Mama."

"Like him? I adore him!"

Felicia gave her a smile. The irony was secret, as was her sadness. But her mother's joy did please her.

"I don't know how you can remain so calm, though," Louisa said. "Being married in two days? I don't understand why you aren't jumping up and down."

"I guess I'm used to the idea, Mama."

Louisa took her daughter's left hand and drew it up for a close look at her ring. "How beautiful! And he picked it out himself. What a man! Do you love it?"

"Yes, Mama, it's very nice."

"Nice is hardly the word, Felicia."

"It's just what I would have picked."

"Then Nick knows your taste. That's a good sign, considering you haven't known each other long. But then, you must know that or you wouldn't be marrying him."

Felicia nodded and handed two of the goblets to her mother. "We'd better get back to the table."

They carried the desserts into the dining room, where the men were sitting in what looked like an uncomfortable silence.

"You haven't lived, Nick," Louisa said, "until you've had Felicia's chocolate mousse."

"If it's anything like her mother's linguini, it will be fabulous," he said.

"Aren't you sweet." She picked up her spoon. "Carlo said he wasn't sure if he married me for my linguini or for my figure. After thirty-six years, I've decided it had better have been for the linguini," she said with a laugh.

"You know perfectly well Papa loves you for yourself," Felicia told her mother.

"Every woman deserves a husband who loves her," Carlo said, his tone serious. He glanced pointedly at Nick. "It's a crime if she gets less."

Felicia looked at Nick, too. If there was guilt in him, he hid it well. She wondered if he'd missed her father's point, but then she realized that Nick might have considered it irrelevant, since he had no inkling of the truth behind the situation.

She took a hasty bite of the mousse but hardly noticed the flavor. She didn't want her father to get started. No telling what he'd say if he let his anger get to him. "There are many kinds of happiness, Pops," she said, hoping to smooth the way to the next topic.

"All I know," Louisa said, reaching over to touch Nick's arm, "is that this is a happy occasion." She turned to her husband. "Isn't it, Carlo?"

He grunted his assent.

"Can I confess one tiny disappointment, though?" Louisa said to Nick. She gave Felicia a sideward glance, then went on. "My joy would be complete if I knew my dear child was being married by a priest."

"Mama, we discussed that," Felicia admonished.

"It's true!" she insisted.

"Don't meddle, Louisa," Carlo said.

"No," Nick interjected, "Mrs. Mauro has a point. Felicia has sacrificed a large family wedding for me, it isn't right that she should give up the blessing of the church, as well. I've been giving it some thought. I'll arrange for a priest to marry us."

Felicia was shocked. "You will?"

"Is it possible?" Louisa added.

"The request will not be popular, given the shortness of the time, but I think one can be persuaded."

"No doubt," Carlo said under his breath.

Felicia looked at her father, but Louisa had already gone off into trills of giddy laughter.

"A prayer come true!" she said, gushing. "Oh, Nick, what a dear sweet boy you are! I'm beginning to think you deserve my angel. Felicia, I see now why you love him!"

The remark brought a smile to Nick's lips. Felicia was coloring even before their eyes met. His brow arched again and he had that same bemused, self-satisfied expression on his face. It was almost as if he was chiding her. "See," he seemed to be saying, "I can be a charmer . . . if I want to be."

What in fact he did say was, "This mousse is delicious, by the way. I see now why you're the queen of desserts."

"Her goal has always been to own a dessert diner," Carlo said somberly. "I hope for her sake marriage will not be the end of that dream."

"Pops," Felicia admonished, "that's just talk."

"Don't listen to her, Mr. Mondavi," Carlo said. "If you marry my daughter, you should know what's in her heart."

"I'm glad you told me," Nick said, sounding sincere, though she knew perfectly well he wasn't. Proof was the look of irony he gave her.

Felicia hated it that he had this power over her, especially considering it was based entirely on a misconception. He thought he was so clever, but he was the one in the dark.

"What are *your* dreams, Mr. Mondavi?" Carlo asked. "I'd like to know what you have in mind for your life with my daughter."

Felicia glared at her father. Why was he pushing? Didn't he know how delicate the situation was?

"My first dream is that she be happy, Mr. Mauro," Nick said. "I promise to do what I can to make that happen."

Carlo gave Nick a long, hard look. Felicia searched desperately for something to say.

"Isn't that the most romantic thing you ever heard?" Louisa intoned, oblivious to the undercurrents. "What a wonderful young man!" She gave Felicia a tearful smile and squeezed Nick's hand. "You'll be happy. I know this in my heart."

"We must go soon, Louisa," Carlo said. "You know what the doctors told us. Too much excitement is not good for my heart."

FELICIA STOOD at the door watching her parents go down the hall, each with a bouquet of roses. When they got to the stairs, her mother glanced back and gave her a wave. Her father looked back, too, but his expression was dour. He was the one she felt sorry for. The whole evening he acted as though he were attending the execution of his only child.

Felicia turned to Nick. A smudge of her mother's lipstick was on his cheek.

"Thank you," she said to him as she closed the door. "Thank you for being so nice to my parents."

"It was the least I could do. A man's got to have a good relationship with his in-laws." He gave her a wink.

"Are you making light of this?"

"It's a wedding, Felicia. No point in treating it like a funeral. Anyway, I'd have thought you'd be glad for a lighter mood."

"I suppose it's better than the opposite."

She went and sat in her grandmother's chair, wanting to keep some distance between them. Nick took the love seat. She tried to decide how she felt about the evening. God knew, it had been a roller-coaster ride emotionally. All during dinner, she'd been so very aware of him. Then, once her parents had come, she'd worried what her father might say or do.

Felicia glanced at Nick. He was silently regarding her. But he had that look on his face again—the look that told her he was thinking what it would be like to make love with her. She fiddled with her fingers.

"Your father hates me," Nick observed mildly. "Did he hate everyone you went out with?"

"He doesn't hate you."

"A man knows what another man is thinking. And he seemed especially concerned that marrying me might be the end of your dream."

"Which dream are you referring to, exactly?"

Nick gave her a wry smile. "The dessert diner. Did you think I meant finding Prince Charming?"

"You don't have to concern yourself with my father, Nick."

"But I do have to concern myself with you. So tell me more about this dream of yours...the restaurant, I mean."

Nick was playing with her. Definitely. She started to let him know she didn't appreciate his little joke, but she stopped herself. She couldn't afford to get into a sparring match with him. Too much was riding on this. Instead she forced a smile.

"I like to cook, as you know, and I've been thinking about opening my own place for a couple of years now."

"And what stopped you?"

"Money, mainly. That and my father's health. He needs me at the restaurant. But I guess he's going to have to get along without me anyway...." Her voice trailed off.

"And you aren't thinking of a full-service restaurant. Just desserts?"

"Yes. Just desserts..." Her eyes lit up. "Just desserts! That's it!"

"What?"

"The perfect name for my restaurant. Just Desserts! Wow! Thanks, Nick!"

"I didn't know I was so clever."

"You must have a hidden talent for irony. It's so fitting."

Nick seemed unsure what she meant. Too bad. The point was, she knew. And maybe, if she was real lucky, she'd eventually see both Nick and his uncle Vinny get their just deserts for what they were doing to her. But that, like her restaurant, was for another day.

"You want more coffee?" she asked, figuring a change of subject was called for.

"No. I should go soon. I know you're tired."

He was right about that. A few hours ago she'd never laid eyes on the man. Now she wore his ring, and in two days she'd be his bride.

She still couldn't believe it was happening. It seemed as though this ought to be a game. Going out with the fat doctor to please her parents would have been a game—not a fun one, but a game. This wasn't. She was giving up her life so her father wouldn't have to give up his.

"Tomorrow I'll make arrangements for the wedding," he said. "Do you have special needs or requests?"

"My mother wants me to wear my wedding dress," she said.

"The one you were going to wear for Johnny Fano?"

"Yes."

"I suppose that's your right."

"You don't like the idea?"

"As long as you're happy."

If it was sarcasm, she wasn't going to call him on it. She had to consider herself fortunate he was being so compliant.

"It would mean renting a tuxedo," she told him.

"Then I'll rent one."

"I'm sorry to ask you to do it."

"Whatever you think of me, Felicia, your mother will still be my mother-in-law and your mother."

"I have no other requests."

"Fine. Then it's settled." He checked his watch. "It's been a nice evening, but I really should go. It's been a long day for us both."

Before he got up, Nick acted as if he wanted to say something more, but he didn't. If she didn't know better, she'd have said he was torn, too. He went to the door. Felicia followed him. He regarded her again.

"As soon as I've made arrangements for the wedding, I'll let you know so you can inform your parents," he said. "As of now, I think we'll come back here after our wedding night and spend the day before flying to New York. You might want to pack and take care of your affairs."

She nodded. "Whatever you say."

She saw the flinty look in his eyes and couldn't tell if it was anger or frustration or both. He looked at her for quite a long time, his expression gradually softening. Finally he gave her a faint smile and let his eyes slowly rake down her.

Felicia lowered her eyes. Nick didn't retreat. The vibrations from him seemed to intensify. He moved closer, then reached out and slipped his hand under her hair, grasping her by the back of the neck.

She looked into his eyes, her heart starting to rock. He drew her to him, his fingers tightening on her nape. Then he lowered his mouth and kissed her.

His lips were surprisingly soft. It was not a demanding kiss, but there was purpose in it. Her body was tense, yet she did not resist. She did not pull away. Her hands touched his arms. She was aware of the heat of his body, his strength, but in spite of that she did not embrace him.

After a few seconds their lips parted. Nick pressed his cheek against hers. His scent filled her nostrils, making her heart lurch.

"It's a start," he said softly, so softly it was almost a whisper. Then, after peering into her eyes, bemused, he went out the door.

NICK DECIDED to walk to the Fairmont on Nob Hill. It was about ten blocks, most of it up a steep hill, but he needed the exercise. And climbing Powell Street was almost like being on a stair climber, especially once he reached the section where the cable cars ran.

As he walked, he thought about Felicia. The last moment had been delicious, but one he'd forced on her. She'd neither shoved him away in anger nor embraced him. The kiss was a reflection of the entire evening. Equivocal. Damn, but the woman confounded him!

He decided it wasn't an act. She was confused. As confused as he was. They both knew she was being paid to marry him—so there was no need for pretense—yet one minute she was acting almost virginal, the next she was telling him she would do whatever he asked of her, including getting her pregnant!

She was a crazy-maker. But for some reason that did not turn him off. Just the opposite. From the first moment he saw her he'd wanted her. It wasn't just that she was beautiful, he was certain of that. Yet he couldn't say what it was that he found so alluring.

The instinct to give in to his desire to kiss her had probably been the right one. There was chemistry between them. That made it easier. And a hell of a lot more pleasant.

In any case, he wasn't going to berate himself over it. What she'd done, she'd done of her own free will. If she didn't want him, she never should have made the deal. Business, after all, was business. Even when complicated by emotions.

Nick arrived at the entrance to the Fairmont, a fine sheen of perspiration on his brow from his walk, despite the coolness of the air. The doorman greeted him.

Nick entered the plush lobby of the grand old hotel. He had his key so he went directly to the bank of elevators around the corner and rode up with a young couple who appeared to be on their honeymoon. They exited the car the floor before his, going off hand-in-hand.

The couple reminded him of his honeymoon. He and Gina had gone to Sardinia, a million miles from San Francisco. But that look of love in the girl's eyes was the same as the one Gina had had for him—unequivocal and uncomplicated. Loving.

As he walked along the corridor, Nick realized that it was a mistake to allow himself to become prisoner to some antiquated romantic ideal. This situation couldn't be more different than when he'd met Gina. He was older, wiser and deeply enmeshed in the troubles of the world now. Felicia had her own troubles and her own agenda. They had little to do with him, except for the accident that he was a buyer and she a seller. Nick realized it was terribly important that he keep a perspective on things.

When he entered his room, he found the message light on. The clerk at the front desk read him the message.

"Mr. Mondavi, please phone me tonight. It doesn't matter how late you get in. I'll wait for your call. Signed Carlo Mauro." The clerk read him the telephone number.

Nick hung up, wondering what that could be about. But if the poor man was waiting to hear from him, he'd better put him out of his misery. He dialed the number. Carlo answered.

"Oh, Mr. Mondavi," he said, "thank you so much for calling."

"What's the problem, Mr. Mauro?"

"You seemed like a decent person," the old man said. "A kind man. For that I am very pleased."

"Thank you," Nick said, not sure where this was leading.

"You said your mother was dead. Can I assume you loved and respected her?"

He was surprised by the question. Carlo's voice indicated he was entirely sincere. "Yes," Nick replied, "I love and honor the memory of my mother very much."

"Then . . ." He hesitated, his voice faltering. "Can I ask that on your mother's grave you swear you will not repeat what I am about to ask you to any living person? No one, not a soul?"

A funny feeling went through him. Nick was as leery as he was surprised. "Okay, I swear I won't repeat what you say."

"On your mother's grave?" Carlo's voice quivered.

"Yes, on my mother's grave."

"All right, Mr. Mondavi, I want to know what amount you want in order to give me back my daughter."

"What?"

"How much money do you want? You name the price and you can have it—as much as I have in this world."

The man's tone was pleading. Nick was shocked.

"Mr. Mauro, I don't think . . ."

"Every man has his price," Carlo interjected. "I have three hundred thousand in cash and stock I've saved for retirement. You can have it all. Is that enough?"

Nick was incredulous. "Mr. Mauro, this isn't about money."

"My restaurant is worth a great deal," Carlo said. "Of course, I must sell it, and that takes time. Unless you will take it yourself. And the cash, too. Everything I have is yours, for my daughter's freedom."

Nick wondered if the hand of Felicia was somehow in this, but he dismissed the notion. A short time earlier she'd been telling him he could do with her as he wished. So were these just the words of a jealous father? Or was it a test?

"Look, Mr. Mauro, I'm not sure what you really want, but—"

"I want my child's life!" Carlo shouted. "Her freedom! There's got to be something you will take for it. Please, I beg you. Just tell me what."

The man's desperation caught Nick totally by surprise. Something more was at play than met the eye. It had to be. "What's going on here, Mr. Mauro? Why are you so upset?"

"I'm trying to save my child," the old man said, on the verge of tears.

"From what? Me?"

"This marriage is not right. You must see that. After tonight I realized you are a decent man. That is why I called you."

"I appreciate the vote of confidence," Nick said, "but you need to talk to your daughter, not me. Nobody's twisting her arm."

There was a long silence. After a while he began wondering if Carlo Mauro was all right.

"Mr. Mauro?"

"I can't do that," Carlo replied wearily. "I mean, I have, but it's no use. I thought as a man of honor you would help."

"Felicia's an adult. She can make her own decisions."

"Then you won't help."

Nick thought. "Talk to Felicia," he said. "If the two of you want to come here in the morning to discuss the matter, I'll listen to what you have to say. That's the best I can do."

Carlo was silent. Then after a time he said, "You may be kind in one way, Mr. Mondavi, but you don't make it easy for me. But I will do it your way. I will talk to Felicia. And in the morning we will come to you."

Nick hung up, wondering what in the hell was going on.

NICK SLEPT later than he'd planned. The first thing he did was order a room-service breakfast. Then he called his aunt in New York.

"Felicia's mother wants us to be married by a priest," he told her. "Would you ask Uncle Vinny to arrange it?"

"I hate to ask because Vinny and the church have always been oil and water," his aunt replied. "But I understand the mother's concern. I would be the same. Yes, I'll see to it."

"Thank you."

"Anything else, Nicky?"

"Aunt Maria, there's something funny going on. Felicia's being paid to marry me, but I don't see that she has much need for money. Do you know what's behind this?"

"No, Nicky. You know your uncle never says what he does, and I never ask."

"You and me both. Well, no problem, I thought maybe he'd have let something slip."

"Not Vinny."

"No, I guess you're right about that. In his business, slips can be fatal."

"Don't talk to me of your uncle's business, Nicky. You know how I feel about that."

"Sorry."

"But don't worry," Maria said, "tell Felicia she will have her priest."

Nick hung up and went to shave and shower. After he'd dried off he put on his trousers in case the room-service waiter arrived. He was about to dry his hair when there was a knock at the door. He went to let the waiter in, but to his surprise it was Felicia. She had a look of consternation on her face.

"Nick, I've got to talk to you."

She entered without waiting to be invited, brushing past him. Turning to face him, she seemed to notice his bare chest and wet hair for the first time.

"Sorry to disturb you," she said, "but I couldn't wait."

"What's wrong?"

"My father was at my apartment at the crack of dawn, wanting me to talk to you. We had a big argument, and he confessed what he'd done."

"You mean that he called me?"

"Yes."

"It was bizarre," he said, "but hardly a criminal act."

"Nick, please forget it happened," she said, drawing near him. "Pops is very emotional about me marrying. He doesn't understand what's happening."

"I'd say that's because you haven't told him the truth. Of course, that may be worse than leaving him to his illusions."

She bit her lip. But instead of acting angry or affronted as she had when money had been mentioned before, her expression turned pleading. "If you'll forget that it happened, and don't tell your uncle, I'll do anything you want."

Nick shook his head in disbelief. "What does my uncle have to do with this? What the hell's going on, Felicia?"

She moved closer, gazing at his chest. Incredibly, there was a seductive look on her face, though there was fear in her eyes. She put her trembling hands on his shoulders. It was only then Nick realized she intended to kiss him.

"It's all my fault," she purred. "I've been sending mixed signals. I thought maybe you'd like it, but I see it was wrong. Please, forget about my father's call. I have only one desire now and that's to make you happy." She leaned forward and kissed his chin. Then she stroked his chest.

Nick felt himself becoming aroused. Felicia amazed him at every turn. Last night when he kissed her she'd been compliant yet aloof—not fighting him, but not giving in, either. Now she seemed ready to take his clothes off.

"Felicia, what's this about?"

She lifted her face and kissed him on the lips. He started to protest, but the sweet taste of her mouth distracted him. She pressed her soft body against him. Nick put his arms around her and gathered her closer. The kiss deepened.

When it was over, he inhaled the rich aroma of her body, waiting for his heart to quiet its erratic beat. He had half a mind to take her to the bed, but then she looked at him with glistening eyes. He saw that desire wasn't driving her. It was anxiety.

"Felicia?"

"I'll be the best wife to you I can, Nick. Just tell me what you want."

He wanted to believe her. But he didn't. She was acting out of desperation, fear. It didn't take a genius to see that.

There was no point pressing for the truth, though, because it was clear he'd never get it. None of this made sense—Uncle Vinny paying her to marry him, her father trying to pay him not to, Felicia's desperation.

"Is this what you want?" she said, pressing her soft breasts against him.

"You're beautiful," he said. "How could I not want you? But..."

"But what?" She ran her hand between their bodies, cupping the bulge in his loins. He hardened even more.

"Would you like to have me now?" she whispered, a tremor going through her as she touched him.

Nick was taken aback. He took both her wrists and held them firmly, at the same time looking into her eyes. "Don't you think this is overdoing things a little?"

"You don't like it?"

He couldn't help a smile. How did he tell her that believing her was more important than having her? He didn't want sex for the sake of sex. And yet, he knew that there was a very real, very definite chemistry between them. Whether Felicia was ready to admit it or not, at some level she wanted him—just as he wanted her. But he couldn't tell her that, either. "You know what I'd really like?" he said.

"What?"

"Dead-on honesty. The truth."

A dark look crossed her face.

"Is it so difficult?" he asked.

"Okay," she said. "The truth is, I came here because I want you to swear you'll never speak to anyone about my father calling you."

"That's it? That's all?"

"Yes."

"That's what this seduction was all about?"

"Yes."

Nick smiled sardonically. "I could have saved you a lot of trouble. All you had to do was ask."

"Then you promise?"

"I promise."

She seemed relieved. "Then everything is all right?"

Nick thought of his arousal, the fact that he'd been ready to jump into bed with her. If it wasn't so painful, it would be funny. "Everything's wonderful," he said.

Felicia smiled. "So what now, Nick?"

"You must have a lot to do to get ready for the wedding and the move to New York. Go on home."

She hesitated. "You're okay with things?"

"Everything's peachy keen, Felicia."

She gave him a quick kiss on the cheek, her eyes shimmering.

"I do have one regret."

"What?"

"I'd like to understand what the hell's going on in that crazy head of yours."

Her expression turned somber. "That's the one thing I can't tell you, Nick."

"Why not?"

She started to turn away, and he grabbed her wrist.

"Why not?" he asked again.

"You can have my body. But you can't have my thoughts. I have to keep something just for me."

She went to the door and opened it. The room-service waiter was there, looking as if he was about to knock. Felicia slipped past him and disappeared down the hall.

The waiter entered. "Your breakfast, sir."

"Thanks."

Nick signed the bill, adding a tip. The man left. Nick poured coffee from the decanter, wondering what the hell Felicia was up to. He had a hunch Uncle Vinny could explain everything, but talking to him would be next to impossible. And dangerous. Besides, he probably wouldn't get a straight answer.

No, this was something he'd have to work through himself. As far as marrying Felicia was concerned, he didn't have many options. She was his best hope of escaping unscathed. And it was damned ironic how he needed her as badly as she seemed to think she needed him.

Whether by accident or design, Felicia Mauro seemed to have his number. But why should he be surprised? Vincent Antonelli, for all his faults and failings, was a genius of sorts. He knew how to make people do things and get results, whether for good or for ill. Somehow, some way, dear old Uncle Vinny had found just the girl to wrap Nick around her finger. And the hell of it was, he was beginning to enjoy it.

# 7

THE DAY BEFORE the wedding they drove up to Lake Tahoe—Felicia, her parents and Nick. He provided the limo. At least she thought he had. For all she knew Vinny Antonelli had made the arrangements, because Nick did admit that the huge estate on the shores of the crystal blue lake where they were to stay was owned by friends of his uncle. Nobody asked what sort of friends. Felicia didn't want to know.

On the drive up, Carlo hardly spoke. Louisa carried the conversation. She and Nick talked a lot about Sicily. Felicia's maternal grandparents were from there, and Louisa had visited the country twice, the last time shortly before Nick was born. But they managed to compare notes just the same.

As it turned out, Nick had needed an extra day to arrange for the priest. The one Vinny found was in Carson City, which meant they'd have to drive over the mountain from Lake Tahoe for the ceremony. Then, after a brief reception, the limo would take her parents back to San Francisco, and she and Nick would spend their wedding night at the lake.

Felicia wasn't sure whether the delay was a blessing or not. When she'd tried on her wedding gown, she discovered it had to be let out a tiny bit in the waist and bust. The extra day gave her mother enough time to make the alterations. It also meant that Felicia had an extra twenty-four hours to wonder and worry about her wedding night.

It seemed as if every waking hour of the past couple of days Nick Mondavi had been on her mind in one way or another. She had often thought about their kiss in her apartment, and again in his hotel room. Both times she'd been torn. He was sexy—no doubt about that. Under normal circumstances, she would have probably loved being in his arms. But the present circumstances were not the least bit normal.

She'd enjoyed making love with Johnny. It seemed as if they could never get enough of each other. Of course, she had been in love. And when she'd gone to bed with other men during the past fifteen years, it was always when *she* wanted to. Even if none of them had been as sexy as Nick, she'd wanted them, and because she had a choice, she'd enjoyed it. Not as much as with Johnny, but it hadn't been something she'd dreaded.

*Choice.* That was the real issue. She had no choice but to marry Nick, and she had no choice but to go to bed with him. And whether she liked making love with him or not, soon he'd have the right to take her again and again and again.

Felicia looked out the window of the limo and shivered, recalling the feel of his chest under her hand as she'd kissed him in his hotel room. Nick had been turned on by her. He'd been fully aroused. And though he'd turned her down, he could have had her right then.

In a way, it might have been better if he had. She'd prepared herself for it—hell, she'd been prepared to do anything that morning if it meant saving her father from Vinny. But as it turned out, giving her a reprieve only meant giving her more time to think about the inevitable.

Felicia's reverie was broken when her mother suggested they stop for a drink at Sam's restaurant in Cameron Park, a town in the foothills. Her father went inside, too, because he wanted to go to the bathroom. She and Nick got out to stretch their legs. The air was hot and dry. They found a shady spot. Nick stared out across the parking lot at the hazy, sunbaked countryside.

"Is everything all right?" she asked.

He seemed surprised by the question. "Sure. Why?"

"You've seemed quiet the past few days," she said.

"Quiet compared to what?"

She saw his point. "Yes, compared to what. Maybe this is the normal you."

"I'm trying to make this as easy for you as I can, Felicia."

"I appreciate that. I truly do."

They watched a large family, including half a dozen small children, come out of the restaurant. Nick smiled at the antics of one of the boys. She saw a sensitivity she hadn't noted before.

"Do you like kids?" he asked.

She flushed, wondering if he was thinking about a baby they might have. For all she knew, he might impregnate her sometime in the next day or so. "I haven't been around them much."

She saw a trace of a smile on his lips, then it was gone. Her parents came out of the restaurant, interrupting their conversation.

They returned to the limo and resumed their trip to Tahoe. Nick wasn't any more talkative than before, though he seemed to be watching her more closely and with what she took to be secret thoughts.

The house where they were staying was on the west shore of the lake. Though fairly modern, it was reminiscent of a French château in that it was made of stone and had spires and turrets, and the various wings seemed to ramble on forever.

Felicia and her parents had a whole guest wing to themselves. Nick stayed in the master suite where, presumably, they'd spend their wedding night. Earlier, as they were driving around the lake, Nick had proposed that they eat out that night, though there was a chef on duty at the estate. He also asked if they'd like to take in a show at one of the casinos at Stateline.

Louisa ventured that the two lovebirds would probably rather be alone—a comment that brought a groan from her father. But Nick quickly insisted that weddings were for families. His folks were gone, why shouldn't his future in-laws be happy? In the end the four of them dined at Harrah's, and Carlo went home afterward to rest his heart. Louisa stayed on at Nick's insistence, and the three of them took in a Tony Bennett show. Louisa adored Tony Bennett.

Nick was going the extra mile for her mother. Felicia appreciated that, even if he did make her nervous during the course of the evening by constantly watching her. She could almost see the secret thoughts streaming though his mind. When he'd touched her, laying his warm hand on her waist as they passed through a doorway or taking her elbow to help her in or out of the limo, she'd felt the energy between them.

They returned to the estate shortly before midnight. Louisa hurried out of the limo, bid them both good-night and went inside.

Felicia lingered outside to watch the stars. Nick stayed with her. The Milky Way was like a bright swath of paint spread across the indigo sky. It was beautiful, romantic. She inhaled the crisp mountain air, knowing that tomorrow at this time she would belong to Nick Mondavi in every sense of the word.

"I hope it hasn't been too tedious for you. I think my mother talked nonstop from San Francisco to Sacramento."

"She's a sweet lady."

"Yes, she is."

They both fell silent. It was a couple of minutes before Nick spoke. "I'm sure you're tired," he said. "Perhaps we should go in so you can go to bed."

"Are you staying up?"

"For a while, maybe. I thought I'd have a nightcap."

"Oh."

"Would you like something?" He said it politely enough, but it came across as an afterthought.

"No, you're right. I should go to bed," she said. "I've got to get up early and bake our wedding cake."

"You're baking a wedding cake?" he asked, as they started toward the front door of the estate.

"Yes, an Italian coconut wedding cake. It's a recipe that's been in my family for years. There have been changes over time, but my mother had it at her wedding, and her mother before that."

"I see."

He opened the door and they stepped inside.

"It's for my mother more than it's for me," she explained.

"Because to you it's not a real wedding?" he said, locking the front door.

She wasn't sure what he was suggesting. "Real enough, I guess." Nick seemed to be deep in thought again, perhaps trying to decide what sort of wife he wanted. Well, she'd find out soon enough.

"What are you thinking?" he asked.

She flushed. "I was wondering what you were thinking as a matter of fact."

"I believe I asked first."

She relented. "I'm a little nervous about tomorrow."

"Brides are supposed to be nervous, Felicia."

She wanted to say, "Yeah, but they aren't supposed to be wondering what's expected of them," but of course, she didn't. Instead she said, "This isn't a normal wedding, and I'm not a normal bride."

"Very true."

She shifted uneasily. Nick waited. Then she said, "Well, I think I'll go to bed now."

Nick reached out and touched her cheek. "Sleep well."

SHE STOOD in the enormous white-tiled kitchen, creaming sugar and butter as the sun rose from behind the mountains on the Nevada side of the lake. Dawn was just breaking when she'd come downstairs and, for the past twenty minutes, she had watched the subtle changes of color in the sky and water as she gathered her ingredients. She wore sweats and running shoes, her favorite attire when she cooked.

At the moment she was adding shortening and beaten egg yolks to the batter. She started the mixer again, blending everything to a creamy consistency. Looking up, she saw her mother.

"I thought I'd find you here," Louisa said. "Worrying more about your cake than your hair." She shook her head. "How many times will you get married, Felicia?"

"Fewer times than I've tried, obviously."

"This is not a day to speak of that," Louisa said, rolling her eyes.

"Why are you giving me a hard time about baking my wedding cake? You did this the morning of your wedding, didn't you?"

"Well, my mother did most of the work. What I did was only to keep busy because I was so nervous."

"Maybe I'm nervous, too, Mama."

"Are you?"

Felicia shrugged. "A little."

"You're something, but I'm not sure nervous is the way I would describe it."

"What do you mean?"

Louisa put her hands on her hips and gave Felicia a level look. "I'll be honest. I have a feeling something's wrong.

I asked your papa if he noticed, but he said I should mind my own business. Is something bothering you?"

The batter was mixed, so Felicia set it aside and measured the flour, soda and salt into a bowl. "There's nothing to worry about," she said as she put the dry ingredients into the sifter.

"Do you love Nick?" Louisa asked as she watched, "or are you putting on an act?"

"What kind of a question is that?"

"A serious one. I sense something is wrong. You and Nick are so formal with each other. Tell me, are you marrying because you are desperate?"

"No, Mama, I'm not."

"At your age it's not so bad to settle. A man doesn't have to be perfect. But that's what has me confused. Nick is so nice and generous, and he's more handsome than Johnny, to say nothing of your father's doctor friend. I'd think you would be thrilled when the alternatives are not so wonderful."

"Mama, a woman my age is more levelheaded about marriage."

"I hope you find more enthusiasm after the ceremony, or your wedding night will be the dullest on record. If you want to know the truth, I feel sorry for Nick. I can tell he loves you."

Felicia blinked. "Oh?"

"Of course. You of all people ought to know."

"Yes, I do," Felicia said uneasily. She put the sifter aside. "It's just interesting that you find it so obvious."

"If the groom doesn't love the woman he's marrying, there's nothing ahead but trouble. Nick is not stupid. Besides, love is on his face. It's you I don't understand." Louisa took her arm. "Tell me, you aren't thinking of Johnny, are you?"

"No, Mama, of course not."

Louisa saw an apron on the counter and put it on. "Let me help. What do you need?"

"You can sift everything two more times," Felicia said, handing her the sifter and bowl.

Felicia went to get the buttermilk from the huge industrial-size refrigerator. She could only imagine the parties that must have been held here. The reception they'd planned would probably be the most modest party on record. Nick ordered champagne, and they'd have cake. Then her parents would head for home, leaving her alone with her new husband.

Only then did she realize her mother had asked her a question. "What, Mama?"

"I said, does Nick want children right away? I haven't wanted to ask him directly."

"It's something we're considering," she replied obliquely.

"Good Catholic boys don't consider such things, Felicia," her mother rejoined, "they just do." She'd finished the second sifting. "I hope Nick realizes you can't wait too long."

"Mama, I don't want to discuss this on my wedding day. Let's change the subject."

"What do you want to talk about then? The weather?"

Felicia ignored the sarcasm. "How's Papa taking things? Is he okay?"

"That's another thing," Louisa said with a frown. "He's wanted you to marry for years. Now that it's happening, he's acting like a man on his way to a funeral."

"Pops is sentimental," she said, putting her hand on her mother's shoulder. "Don't give him a hard time. Just love him and understand."

"How can I understand what makes no sense?" Louisa said, handing Felicia the bowl of thoroughly sifted flour. "There is something I'm not being told. That I'm sure about."

"Please, Mama, just try to enjoy the day."

Felicia took the dry ingredients and added the buttermilk, then mixed that with the creamed mixture she'd set aside earlier. She measured the coconut while her mother began chopping the pecans finely, without being asked.

In the past fifteen years Felicia had only made the cake twice—for her cousin Julie's wedding and for the wedding of a friend. It was not a traditional wedding cake in either America or Italy, but it was distinctive and rich and...well, sensuous. Sensuous food somehow went with Nick.

Louisa had given up and began talking about her own wedding. The story had been oft told, so Felicia only had to listen with half an ear. Her nervousness took her back to another wedding day—her first.

At the rehearsal dinner, Johnny had acted very nervous. In retrospect she understood why, but at the time she assumed it was just wedding jitters. She'd been so naive. The morning of that wedding day, she thought she'd go to bed as Felicia Fano. Who'd have imagined that fifteen years later the cake and dress would be the same, but the groom would be different?

"Nuts are chopped," Louisa announced.

Felicia checked to make sure they were chopped fine enough. As a cook she was a perfectionist. Taking the bowl, she added the nuts and the coconut to the batter, plus a touch of vanilla.

"Egg whites next?" her mother said.

"Yes."

"I'll beat them," Louisa said. "And yes, I know, nice and stiff."

As her mother beat the eggs, Felicia went over to the large window overlooking the lake. She saw a sailboat a quarter of a mile or so out on the placid water, its bright red sail in sharp contrast to the crystalline blue of the lake.

Absently wiping her hands with a towel, she saw some movement down by the dock.

It was Nick. He was rigging a small sailboat. A little surge of excitement went through her at the sight of him. But then she caught herself. This was not the man she loved. What was she thinking?

And yet, despite herself, she was affected by the sight of him. Nick had wormed his way into her mind. In fact she'd dreamed about him the night before. Her memory was fuzzy, but she had a recollection of being tied up. Which made sense. In a figurative sense, Nick *had* her tied up. She was his to do with as he wished. She was ashamed to admit it, but the notion fascinated her.

Whether he fully appreciated the power he had over her, she couldn't say. He had to be aware of it—though it might not have pleased him the way it would other men. She couldn't forget that he had been happily married once. This experience had to pale in comparison with that. Though she hadn't given it much thought, Nick could be suffering, too.

He climbed into the small boat and pushed off. Felicia was disappointed. She didn't like admitting it—even to herself—but she liked watching him. Over the past few days she'd come to appreciate his magnetism. Nick intrigued her, though she knew feeling that way was dangerous.

She had to remember that she was vulnerable. If she felt any kind of attraction at all, it was perverse, mindless. She told herself to think of her father. That put everything into perspective.

"How are these egg whites?" her mother asked. "Do they meet with the master chef's approval?"

Felicia went over and took a look in the mixing bowl. "Perfect," she said, giving her mother a kiss on the cheek. "Keep this up and you'll be good at it soon."

"Don't get cheeky with me, young lady. More than one girl's been taken down a notch or two on her wedding day."

Felicia laughed, taking the mixing bowl. "Yes, I remember you insisting I was giving up on Johnny too soon when I wanted to send the guests home...what was it, four hours after the wedding was supposed to begin?"

Louisa shook her head. "When he didn't come, I was sure he'd turn up in a hospital room, unconscious."

Felicia chuckled. "Mama, that's exactly what he was afraid of." She folded in the egg whites as her mother started greasing and flouring the baking pans.

"I'm glad you can laugh about it," Louisa said, "but it was the worst day of our lives."

"I think I can safely agree with that."

"We can look back now and say maybe it was for the better."

"Think so, Mama?"

"I hope you do. For Nick's sake, as well as yours."

"Nick and I understand each other," Felicia told her. That was more an attempt to give comfort than to lie. At least that's what she wanted to believe.

Louisa started on the third pan. "Will you call me from New York and tell me how it's going?"

"Sure, Mama."

"I mean really tell me."

Felicia nodded. "I'll really tell you." She waited until her mother had finished the last pan. "You know I always try to make the best of whatever situation I'm in."

Just then a voice came from behind them. "What are you two going on about?" It was Carlo. "Who's making breakfast? Me?"

"Sit down and rest your heart, Carlo," Louisa said, glancing over her shoulder at him. "What do you want? Something special for the day of your daughter's wedding?"

"Coffee and toast," Carlo said gruffly as he shuffled in his slippers toward the small table at the far end of the room.

"Toast and coffee? That's it?"

"My only daughter is marrying, isn't she? What do you expect? That I want champagne?"

Felicia shook her head with amusement as her parents exchanged barbs. It had been like that between them for as long as she could remember. She divided the batter evenly between the pans and put them in the oven. In about half an hour, they'd be done. While she waited, she'd make the frosting and clean up.

The prattle continued as she took the bowls to the sink. Glancing down at the lake, she noticed Nick had gone maybe fifty yards from shore. He seemed to be looking toward the house. On an impulse she waved. Nick didn't respond. Maybe he wasn't looking her way. His mind might have been a million miles away.

As she stood there observing, his boat found the wind and began moving farther out into the lake. He wouldn't be seeing her now. She sighed wistfully. It made her wonder what their marriage would be like. Would Nick be going his separate way, ignoring her, or would they do things together? Except for what he considered important for appearances' sake, what incentive did he have to be with her? And how did she feel about that, really?

NICK SLICED another piece of cake, licking the frosting from his fingers. God, it was delicious.

Felicia had gone outside with her parents to say a private goodbye. Nick took a gulp of champagne and contemplated the rich hues of the setting sun reflected in the mountains on the Nevada side of the lake. This was his fourth glass, and he was feeling it. The high was pleasant. Champagne gave him a headache, but right now he was feeling good. Hard as it was to believe, he was actually married. Again.

It seemed sacrilegious to compare this to his wedding with Gina. That wedding day had been filled with love and excitement and expectation. This one had not been like that. Not that it had been dreadful, exactly.

Felicia was a beautiful bride. When she'd descended the staircase that morning, his mouth had sagged open, and he'd felt a tremor in his heart at the mere sight of her. But then, a bride, any bride, was special. And Felicia was a very beautiful woman. She had taken his breath away.

Carlo, who'd sullenly waited with him, wiped his eyes at the sight of her. Nick had been too taken aback to speak. Her mother had jumped into the breach.

"It's probably bad luck to see her before the wedding," Louisa said, "but what do you think, Nick?"

"I've never seen a prettier bride," he said simply.

Felicia was not exactly glowing with happiness, but she put on a show for her parents. And he'd done his best, as well.

"I'll say a special prayer to take care of bad luck," Louisa said. "And because you got a priest for the ceremony, God will be pleased. How could He allow bad luck after such kindness?"

"If I'd known you were concerned, I could have rented a car and gone to the church separately," he'd told her.

"No, it's better if we're together," Louisa said quickly. "Then we all arrive at the same time. But if you don't mind, maybe you can ride in the front with the driver," Louisa said. "Coming home, Carlo and I will sit in front so you can have your wife to yourself."

Nick was just as glad to be in the front. Felicia's dress took up most of the rear seat. Her mother had to wedge herself into the opposite corner. Carlo took the jump seat across from them, somber as ever.

From the start, it hadn't promised to be an easy day for any of them. Father Edwards had called him the previous morning and said that he'd respect the bishop's wishes and marry them without proper counseling, but he had to speak with them in private before the ceremony.

That had been difficult for Felicia. Her hands trembled the whole time. She did not lie easily—though maybe she found it even harder to be untruthful with a priest. They could both tell that Father Edwards didn't like the task given him, but to some degree the conversation put his mind at ease, if not theirs.

At Louisa's insistence, Felicia had walked down the aisle of the empty church on her father's arm. The wedding march had a sadly hollow sound, though that was probably more in Nick's mind than in fact.

Felicia didn't look at him as she approached the altar. She had said her vows in a soft voice but with a quiet determination.

Nick was content. Felicia might be his wife now, but he'd had only one marriage that had meant anything. This could only reinforce the sanctity of his vows with Gina, whether her death had ended it or not.

Nick finished the cake, licking his fingers again. He heard someone behind him. Felicia, still in her wedding gown. He saw her as for the first time once more. Oddly, that had happened more than once since the ceremony. He would look at her and tell himself, *She is my wife. This woman is my wife.*

"You like it?" she said.

Nick wiped his fingers on a napkin. "Yes, delicious."

She made her way toward him. She seemed more tentative now that her parents were gone. Maybe she was nervous.

There was color in her cheeks. He didn't know if it was because of the outdoor air or the fact that these were their first moments together alone.

Noticing the glass of champagne she'd put down before going to see her parents off, she picked it up and took a sip. "Well, that's over."

"Were we convincing?"

"Convincing enough." She chuckled. "My mother thinks you love me, so I guess *you* were convincing."

"I'm glad."

She gave him a penetrating look. "Are you?"

"It was my gift."

"Thank you for doing it."

Nick gave a helpless shrug. Felicia took another sip of champagne. He looked her over, aware of the slim bodice of her gown, her breasts, her mouth. When her eyes engaged his, he picked up his flute, fingering it. He saw her hands tremble.

"So, what kind of frosting is this?" he asked.

"Nothing fancy. Butter, cream cheese, a little vanilla and lots of powdered sugar."

"The diet special."

"How often does a person marry?"

"True," he said.

She took a sip of champagne. Nick wasn't usually at a loss for words, but he was now.

"I guess what matters now is the immigration service," she said.

"Yes, the good old INS."

"I'll smile for them whenever they come around."

Nick took a long drink of champagne.

"So, did today give you sad thoughts about your first marriage?" she asked.

He was surprised by the insightfulness of the question. "I thought about it, yes."

The woman who'd set things up for their reception came into the room, but seeing them, turned and started to leave.

"Did you want to clean up?" Nick asked, stopping her.

"I don't mean to interrupt," she replied. "I can clean in the morning. I did want to tell you I'll be leaving shortly."

"I think we're through," he said. "You want more cake, Felicia?"

She shook her head.

Nick motioned for the woman to enter. "It's all yours."

He took the bottle of champagne and filled their glasses as the woman put the dirty dishes and extra glasses on a tray.

"I'll put the rest of the cake in the fridge," she said.

"Good," he said, "we can have it for breakfast." He smiled at Felicia, who was solemn-faced until he looked at her, then she smiled in return.

"To be honest, it's always better the second day."

Nick took her arm, and they went over to the large picture window that afforded a sweeping view of the lake. Twilight was falling. Felicia seemed nervous. It was like the first day at her apartment.

Neither spoke. They stared out at the lake.

"Where did you get married last time?" she asked.

"In Italy. The village where Gina was from. A place called Mistretta."

"Was she beautiful?"

"Not so pretty as you on the outside, but she had an inner glow that was radiant."

"You must have loved her very much."

"I did," Nick said, gulping more champagne.

"You must hate the thought of me taking her place, even if it's only in name."

Nick shook his head, but the only part he knew he didn't mean was the hate. There was nothing about Felicia he hated. He could not blame her. Not for anything. He didn't have to do this, and they both knew it.

Perhaps what bothered him most was the secret pleasure he felt at having her with so little effort on his part and scarcely any commitment. The primary burden was falling on her. That was the part that really bothered him.

As Felicia stared at the darkening waters, he let his eyes wander over her, aware again of the fit of her dress at the waist and bust. The full skirt hid the sensuous curve of her hips, but he could easily picture her legs under the dress.

"What happened to her?" Felicia asked. "You never said."

It took him a moment to reconstruct the conversation and realize she was asking about Gina. "She was hit by a runaway truck as she walked along the sidewalk near our place in Gramercy Park."

"Oh, how terrible."

"The worst was that she four months pregnant at the time."

"Oh, God."

"That's not something I want to talk about. Not today."

Felicia gave him a genuine look of compassion, touching his arm. It eased the momentary pain, though of course he'd learned to deal with it over the years. The first months it had been almost too much to bear. But that was behind him.

"How about you? Did putting on that dress bring on sad thoughts?"

"That's something I don't want to talk about, either."

Nick slowly nodded. "So, here we are, two people, not wanting to talk about the past." He was tempted to add, *And stuck having to deal with each other,* but he didn't. It would have been more to acknowledge her predicament, not his.

He realized that what he wanted was to feel something positive, happy. No, more than that, he wanted to feel something positive and happy with Felicia, this pretend wife of his. Truth be known, he didn't want to pretend.

The attraction he felt was real enough. He wanted the rest to be real, too.

Felicia stared off wistfully. Nick watched her—maybe examined her was the better word. Once more he saw her with fresh eyes. Her cheeks, the lines of her jaw and neck, were perfect. Good bones, fine features, great skin.

He had a sudden, strong desire to possess her, taste her skin, touch her body. He'd been attracted to her from the first, but this was the most powerful urge yet. His heart pounded and he felt perspiration form on his brow. Was it the champagne? The conversation? The knowledge that she was his?

There was something about knowing she was his wife that he found incredibly arousing. During the drive back from Carson City he'd thought of taking her to bed, of consummating what the priest had sanctioned. The words "to love, honor and cherish" had been mumbled by rote. And yet the consequence was that she was his. Beautiful, lovely, Felicia was his, bought and paid for...a wife in whatever sense he chose for that to mean.

"It's getting dark," she said.

Was there an ominous implication in her tone? He looked out, seeing that it was indeed dark. The woman who'd been cleaning was gone. They were alone.

"Are you tired?" he asked.

She turned to face him, as if steeling herself. "You mean, do I want to go to bed?"

"I guess that wasn't very subtle, was it?"

"Are you asking me what I want, Nick?"

There was a firmness to her tone. He wasn't sure whether she was nervous or upset or merely being businesslike.

"I guess I was trying to be polite," he said.

"I think honesty is what's needed now."

"Then let's get one thing clear," he said, annoyed that she'd turned it into a negotiation. "I'm not a rapist."

"Then you do want sex. That's fine," she said. "I just wanted to know."

Nick shook his head. "This is doing wonders for the mood. I hope you realize that."

"I'm sorry. I've been feeling very anxious."

"You expected an announcement?"

"Look, Nick, I said I'm sorry," she said, taking his hand. "Let's go upstairs."

Oddly enough, her compliance was only making it worse. But he didn't say anything. He kept his feelings to himself.

# 8

By the time they reached the master suite, they were both breathing heavily. It was partly the altitude and the climb up the stairs, but it was also fear. She was determined to hide it, but even though she'd thought of little else the last few days, Felicia wasn't really prepared for this.

She still had hold of Nick's hand when she turned to face him in the middle of the bedroom. The light was dim. One small lamp burned in a corner, casting a shadow over Nick's face. His expression struck her as severe. She smiled, even as her chest continued to heave.

Nick stood still. He seemed to be judging her, placing the burden on her. She moved closer to him. She could feel the heat of his body. A fine sheen of perspiration shone on his forehead and lip as he continued drawing long, deep breaths. He neither spoke nor moved.

Felicia touched his chest, the heat of his body coming right through his tuxedo shirt, warming her palm. His rich, masculine aroma rose from him, arousing her, despite her uncertainty.

There was no evil in Nick's eyes, but neither was there friendliness. She did see desire. She slid her hand through the gap in his shirt, between the mother-of-pearl studs, and caressed his chest. He did not move. But when she looked into his eyes she could tell that this was what he wanted. He wanted her even though she wasn't Gina.

Nick ran his finger along her neckline, over the top of her breasts. Her breathing had returned to normal, but his touch sent her heart tripping.

# PLAY
## HARLEQUIN'S

# LUCKY HEARTS
# GAME

## AND YOU GET

- ★ **FREE BOOKS**
- ★ **A FREE GIFT**
- ★ **AND MUCH MORE**

**TURN THE PAGE AND
DEAL YOURSELF IN**

# PLAY "LUCKY HEARTS" AND YOU GET . . .

★ **Exciting Harlequin Temptation® novels—FREE**

★ **PLUS a Beautiful Porcelain Trinket Box—FREE**

# THEN CONTINUE YOUR LUCKY STREAK WITH A SWEETHEART OF A DEAL

1. Play Lucky Hearts as instructed on the opposite page.
2. Send back this card and you'll receive brand-new Harlequin Temptation® novels. These books have a cover price of $3.50 each, but they are yours to keep absolutely free.
3. There's no catch. You're under no obligation to buy anything. We charge nothing — ZERO — for your first shipment. And you don't have to make any minimum number of purchases — not even one!
4. The fact is thousands of readers enjoy receiving books by mail from the Harlequin Reader Service. They like the convenience of home delivery...they like getting the best new novels before they're available in stores...and they love our discount prices!
5. We hope that after receiving your free books you'll want to remain a subscriber. But the choice is yours — to continue or cancel, anytime at all! So why not take us up on our invitation, with no risk of any kind. You'll be glad you did!

Nick took her jaw in his hand and kissed her firmly on the mouth. He tasted of champagne. Sugar from the frosting was on his lips. He held her tightly, crushing her.

The certainty of what was happening scared her. It had been a long time since she'd been with a man. She wasn't prepared for this, either physically or emotionally, but she knew it was going to happen anyway. Vinny had made it her job to make it happen.

By the time the kiss ended they were both breathing hard. Her body was reacting affirmatively, which surprised her. Nick was sexy and handsome, but it wasn't that she was responding to, it was his repressed passion, the heat and cold of his sexuality. It lured her more than it repelled her. It made her want him.

He was palming her breasts through her bodice. Through her fear, a desire was building to give herself to him. It was not rational. It had nothing to do with the deal. And it was only partly sexual. But Felicia realized she wanted to relinquish control, control of her body.

She almost asked him to take her, but words seemed inappropriate, so she said nothing. She stood very still as he leaned over and kissed the top of her breasts, his hands cupping her buttocks through the fullness of her skirts.

Nick kissed her again, and she moaned as their tongues entwined. She took his head in her hands, pressing her mouth hard against his, not understanding the feelings that were raging out of control, feelings that were stronger than she, feelings that followed years of abstinence.

She remembered her cousin Julie telling her that on her wedding night Dominick had made love to her the first time with her wedding dress still on. He'd thrown her down on the bed and ravished her. Hearing about it, Felicia had thought it barbaric, but now she understood perfectly.

She ran her fingers through Nick's hair, pulling on it as she pressed her hips against his. "Do you want me?" she whispered, poking her tongue into the shell of his ear.

"Yes, I want you," he grumbled, sounding faintly angry.

Strangely, the response incited her. "With my dress on?"

He pulled back to look at her, his face registering surprise. "Is that what you want?"

"Yes," she said, not knowing why. Unless it was because when Julie had told her about her wedding night, the wickedness had secretly appealed to her.

Felicia felt wanton. Perhaps it was a need to purge herself, to put her self-imposed celibacy behind her. But she wanted him to take her and be done with it. Now!

Freeing herself from his arms, she went to the bed, a huge king-size affair on a platform. She threw herself onto it, her arms out to the sides. Nick took his time coming to her. Her sudden, impetuous act seemed to have taken him by surprise. Standing by the bed, he looked at her.

"Come on, Nick," she said breathlessly.

He slowly took off his tuxedo jacket and tossed it aside. She watched him remove his bow tie, the studs from his shirt and his cuff links. He took off the shirt, and she gazed at his broad, furry chest. For the first time, her eagerness was tempered with doubt. But she told herself he was going to take her eventually, so it might as well be now, when she was feeling feverish and her head was light from the champagne.

Nick kicked off his shoes, then removed his trousers and socks. She saw the bulge in his undershorts and the covetous expression on his face. He meant to accommodate her.

Felicia closed her eyes. She didn't open them when he removed her shoes. Or when Nick took the hem of her dress and lifted it. The next sensation she felt was the silk of the gown settling on her face. Knowing she was exposed to him, her heart began to rage.

Nick took the tops of her thigh-high white lace stockings and peeled them off. Under the shroud of skirts she couldn't see him, but she imagined him looking at her. When he put his hands on her thighs, drawing his palms along her skin, she shuddered. Part of her wanted to push down her skirts so she could see, but the other part of her wanted, craved, the anonymity.

She lay very still as he reached under her skirts and grasped the waistband of her panties. Lifting slightly so he could remove them, she nevertheless groaned with uncertainty as he pulled the fabric down her legs and off.

Knowing he was looking at her, Felicia felt a rush of warm liquid from her core, a tremor in her stomach and the caress of the cool air between her legs. She moaned.

When Nick parted her knees, she nearly jumped, but she willed herself to remain compliant. She had initiated this dance, giving him what she'd promised, and she had to see it through.

She felt him settle on the bed and his hands moving up the insides of her thighs. Her breath caught, and she clutched the bedspread, struggling to keep from trembling.

His warm breath washed over her skin an instant before his moist lips touched the top of her thighs. He spread kisses over her, around her mound, making her insides throb.

When he touched her there, an involuntary sound rose from her throat. She was so wet his finger easily slid into her opening and up the underside of her nub, sending jolts of excitement through her.

"Oh, God," she moaned, her voice pleading, the air under the skirts hot from her heavy breathing.

Nick opened her legs wider, and she felt his weight settle on her. He entered her then, his size shocking her. Instinctively she wrapped her legs around him. His face was just inches from hers, but the fabric was a veil separating them. She could hear the urgency of his breathing, the force of his breath pushing the silk against her face.

But the fire was between her legs. She arched against him, forcing him deeper. Her excitement built quickly. She felt her climax coming. His groans told her he was there. When he heaved against her forcefully, she came, the pulsing sensation rippling through her body.

Felicia gasped for air, pulling her dress off her face. She found herself staring into his eyes, his expression tortured with ecstasy. They were both breathing hard, struggling to recover. Nick almost looked surprised. Or maybe she was projecting.

Lowering his head, he kissed her mouth. She did not close her eyes. She realized then, at that moment, that she'd just made love to a stranger.

Nick noticed her wariness. "Did I hurt you?" he murmured.

She shook her head. "No."

He lifted himself onto his elbows. "Are you all right?"

"Yes."

Nick looked embarrassed, perhaps because of her reaction. The ecstasy was gone. She felt ashamed. She wanted him to get off her.

He seemed to read her thoughts. As he got up, she pushed her dress down to cover herself. Nick picked up his clothes, giving her an uncertain look.

"Sure you're all right?"

"Yes, I'm fine."

His expression, his body language, clearly told her he didn't believe her. She knew she had to reassure him.

"I hope it was okay for you," she said.

"How could it not be?"

It was an ambiguous response. Was he saying sex was sex? Or was he saying she was wonderful?

"I'm glad."

"You did your job, if that's what you're worried about. Very, very well." Then, tossing his clothes on a chair, Nick went to the bathroom.

Felicia lay staring at the ceiling. She didn't begin crying right away. The tears came slowly, running from the corners of her eyes into her hair. She sobbed a few times and she was through. She would cry again, probably, but not a lot. It would be a long time, however, before the pain went away. But at least the uncertainty was over. Now she knew what it meant to be Nick Mondavi's wife.

WHEN NICK AWOKE in the middle of the night, it took a few moments to remember where he was. Then it all came together—California, not New York. A wife named Felicia, not Gina. Yes, he was married again. And there was something distinctly tragic about that. He felt a dull pain.

His most vivid image of his new wife was her eyes peering at him over the hem of her dress after they had sex. He'd seen dismay, a touch of horror and maybe hatred. Quiet, quiet hatred.

He listened for the sound of her breathing, but couldn't hear it. Earlier, after he'd returned from the bathroom, she'd gone in to take a shower, returning to bed and quietly slipping under the covers. She hadn't dried her hair. He'd smelled the dampness of it, and the scent of perfumed soap. He'd had a strong urge to take her into his arms and hold her then, but he hadn't. It was the sort of intimacy she might have rejected—not sex, but real affection. Nick could be many things, but it was hard for him to be a hypocrite.

He couldn't hold her, so he wanted to smell her as he had earlier—take in the scent of her wet hair and the perfumed soap on her scrubbed skin. Rolling onto his back, he drew a deep breath, but he could smell neither her hair nor the soap. And so he listened to the night.

Outside the wind rose in the pines, moaning. He heard something else, as well. The plaintive whimper of a cat, though it almost sounded like a child. Or a woman.

More fully awake, Nick sat up and looked toward the sliding glass doors that opened onto the deck. In the faint light he could see the curtains billowing. Then he saw that Felicia's side of the bed was empty. The sound coming from outside was her. Was she crying?

If so, they were quiet sobs. He lay down. The crying ceased, but after a minute it started again. He got out of bed, slipped on his robe and went to the glass doors.

The air was fresh with the smell of pine. Pushing aside the curtains, he looked out and saw her in the corner of the deck, curled up in a lounge chair, her bathrobe glowing white in the light of the moon. She was on her side, her knees pulled up to her chest, her hands clasped to her breast. There was nothing as wrenching as a child or a woman crying. He stepped onto the deck.

Felicia saw him immediately and sat upright. He couldn't see her face clearly, but her body language suggested wariness.

"Are you all right?" he asked.

"Yes," she answered.

He approached the lounge chair. "I heard you crying. I thought . . ."

"It's nothing. I was just feeling a little sad. It was an emotional day."

He didn't believe her. Whatever was wrong, she was dismissing it too easily.

The deck under his bare feet was cold, but he ignored it and pulled the flaps of the robe over his chest. "Is a woman crying on her wedding night supposed to be normal?"

"I wouldn't know," she said after hesitating.

"Somehow I think not."

"If I disturbed you, I'm sorry."

"You didn't. I was awake and I heard you." He could see her face well enough to tell that her expression was impassive. "Are you sure you don't want to talk about it?"

She stared at him but said nothing.

"Felicia?"

"No, Nick, I don't want to talk about it."

He wasn't sure if that meant she didn't or she really did. Gina had a tendency to say the opposite of what she truly meant, forcing him to probe until she gave in and finally spit it out. They'd had a loving relationship, but half the time he didn't understand her.

"You didn't like—" he hesitated, thinking better of what he was going to say, but realized it was too late "—the sex."

"That has nothing to do with it."

There was no conviction in her voice.

"You sure?"

"Look, Nick, you wanted to make love and we made love. But I asked you once before not to ask me what I'm thinking. My body is yours, but I've got to have something. Let me have my thoughts. Please."

Felicia's speech was revealing. Even if he didn't know exactly what was bothering her, he understood the character of the problem.

"That's fair," he said.

She was silent. He got to his feet.

"Why don't you come inside? It's cold out here."

"I don't want to disturb you."

"You won't."

"I'll stay here a few more minutes."

"Whatever you want," he said and headed for the door.

"Nick," she called before he went inside.

"Yes?"

"You aren't mad at me, are you?"

"Why should I be mad at you?"

"I'm not trying to be difficult," she said.

"I'm not accusing you of anything, Felicia. I just don't like thinking I hurt you."

"You didn't."

He knew it wasn't true. This was the price of a marriage made without love. A wife who'd been bought was a wife in name only. But why was he surprised? He'd known that was the way it would be from the very beginning. He just wished it didn't hurt so much.

# 9

NICK WAS SURPRISED to discover that she'd awakened first. In fact, the sound of the shower running woke him up. He put on his robe and went into the master bath just as she was coming out of the shower stall, surprising her.

"Oh," she said, looking alarmed.

"Good morning," he said, handing her a towel.

Felicia took it, holding it in front of her and waiting to see what he would do.

"I apologize for intruding," he said.

She shook off his apology, drying her face with the end of the towel. "That's all right. We're married." She seemed to say the last more to herself than him.

Nick was very aware of her naked body behind the towel. Felicia was aware he was aware, but maintained her modesty.

"I'll use the bath down the hall," he said quickly, grabbing his shaving kit and leaving before she could say another word.

By the time he'd finished and returned to the master suite, Felicia was downstairs. He quickly dressed and went down to find her.

She was in the kitchen. She greeted him with a smile, looking radiant in a white T-shirt and jeans. Her hair was pulled back in a ponytail, and she wore less makeup than ever before. It was a fresh, clean image. The wholesomeness appealed to him.

"Eggs?" she said. "How do you like them? Bacon's bad for your heart, but I'll make some if you insist. There's a carton of that no-cholesterol, no-fat egg stuff in the fridge. I can scramble that for you, if you like."

"That would be great."

She wouldn't let him help, explaining it was a matter of professional pride. So he sat down and watched her, thinking of the night before, regretting what had happened and remembering it fondly at the same time. He had aroused her physically, though he'd failed to satisfy her emotionally. That was the bottom line.

Maybe that made him a bastard. She'd almost certainly regarded him that way. But what alternative did he have—apart from treating her like a roommate? Chances were she'd never think of being his wife as anything but a job, though he couldn't help wondering if someday they might get past all that.

They were on a tight schedule and had to hurry to catch their flight to San Francisco. After breakfast Nick carried their bags to the front door, then went to the kitchen for a mug of coffee to take with him on the drive to the airport. Felicia had told him she didn't want any, but he could see her eyeing the steaming cup just the same.

"Have a sip," he said as they pulled through the gate.

"No, thanks."

"Have some. I'm willing to share."

She took a drink, perhaps to shut him up. Nick looked at her jeans-clad legs, remembering their lovemaking. All his positive, lustful thoughts were a good sign. A man's feelings about a woman the morning after were always a dead giveaway. On many an occasion an attractive woman somehow lost her luster by light of day. But if anything, he liked Felicia better now—though it was more than likely that feeling was not mutual.

At the airport he got her a cup of coffee of her own, and she seemed embarrassed that he was waiting on her.

"You should let me do that," she protested.

"You're not my slave, you know," he replied.

In response, she gave him the strangest look. It wasn't calculated. It was spontaneous and full of incredulity—as if to say, "If not your slave, what then?"

"Maybe this is something we need to talk about," he said.

"Why?" she said. "I think we understand each other."

"Do we? This may not be your normal marriage, but I'd like some semblance of honesty."

"I do the best I can," she said. "That's all you can ask."

They sat sipping coffee for a long time without talking. She seemed at a loss. He decided maybe he needed to be more direct. So he asked the question that had been eating at him for the past couple of days.

"So tell me, how much did my uncle give you to marry me?"

She blinked. "Do you really want to know?"

"Is it embarrassingly a lot, or embarrassingly a little?"

"A lot from my perspective."

"Hmm." He gulped the last of his coffee. "What if I gave you the same amount to be open and honest with me about all your feelings?"

"What are you trying to prove, Nick?"

"Seriously. I want to know what you think."

"First, it wouldn't be worth what it would cost you. And second, I wouldn't tell you even if you did pay me."

"Why?"

"Because you may own me, but you can't have my thoughts."

"You've said that before. It's your trump card, isn't it?"

"Yes, Nick. And it will always be."

That was as close as she'd come to telling him where to get off. And it did tell him where her limits were. He could have her body, but not her heart. Of course, he already knew that.

But why? There was no doubt in his mind that there was real chemistry between them. Felicia had responded to him every time he'd kissed her and when they'd made love. Yet something made her hold back. Probably the same something that had made Carlo offer to pay him to forget about marriage and had made Felicia beg him to forget about her father's offer.

The flight back was brief. An hour after leaving Tahoe they were on the James Lick Freeway in San Francisco, the skyline of the city opening up before them as they came around Hospital Curve. Felicia sighed. It wasn't too hard to figure why. This was her town, and they were leaving it for his.

"Are you going to hold it against me for taking you away from here?" he asked.

"Yes," she said. "San Francisco's been my home for thirty-five years. I'll miss my parents, the restaurant. Leaving is the worst part, if you want to know the truth."

"You can come back for visits. As often as you like."

She glanced at him. "You have a generous streak in you, Nick, don't you?"

"It's just a streak," he said with a laugh. "Normally I'm able to keep it under control."

They were making light of it, but he knew she appreciated his gesture. That made him wonder if Felicia was appreciative by nature, or if it was part of her job description. Vinny wouldn't have been shy about giving detailed instructions. He'd probably even put conjugal arrangements in the contract! Well, Nick would find out in due course. But there was one matter he wanted to deal with now, before they left San Francisco.

"If you don't mind, I'll drop you off at your apartment and take care of an errand," he told her. "I assume you can manage without me."

"Sure," she said, "I'm packed. All I have to do is close the place. Mama will be there next week when the movers come to put the furniture in storage. We've got it all arranged."

The taxi got off the freeway at Seventh Street and followed it up to Market. Skirting the Civic Center, they went north on Leavenworth, through the Tenderloin, up and over Russian Hill, all the way to Filbert.

When the taxi got to her place, Nick climbed out so she wouldn't have to get out on the street side. He offered her his hand, which she took. An awkward moment followed. It was apparent she wasn't sure what to say. Had this been a normal marriage, a bride would have kissed her new husband goodbye, but there'd be no pain in this parting. That went without saying.

Still, Nick didn't let go of her hand, keeping a firm grip until it became obvious. The ocean breeze blew strands of hair across her face. She waited, looking into his eyes.

"I hate to sound sentimental," he said, struggling to keep a straight face, "but this will be our first separation."

"I'm sure the marriage will survive it," she replied. There was a touch of sarcasm in her tone, but maybe amusement, too.

She returned his gaze. He had an exceedingly strong desire to kiss her, to possess her at any cost. He smiled. "Let's hope so."

"See you later, then," she said.

"I'd say half an hour to an hour, max."

Felicia nodded, brushing the loose wisps of hair from her eyes. "I'll be ready."

He watched her walk to the door of her building, appreciating her lovely figure, the flattering fit of her jeans. Once she was inside, Nick climbed into the taxi and told the driver to take him to the Mauros' restaurant. They arrived in a couple of minutes. Nick paid the driver and got out.

Inside he found Carlo Mauro alone at a corner table. There was a stack of menus in front of him, a pad of paper with a list scratched on it. The place was empty. Carlo looked up at the sound of footsteps, then craned his neck to see past him.

"Felicia's finishing with the packing," Nick said, knowing he was wondering if she was with him. "We'll be swinging by your home on the way to the airport so she can say goodbye. In an hour or so."

Carlo nodded, then gave him a so-what-do-you-want look and said, "Is there a problem?"

"Yes. I'd like to talk to you about it."

Carlo calculated. "All right. You want a cup of coffee?" He pushed the menus aside and started to get up.

"No," Nick said. "Thanks, but I don't want anything." He slipped into the booth.

They exchanged looks. Carlo's expression remained sullen, but there was a hint of concern in his eyes, as well. He waited.

"I know you didn't want me marrying Felicia," Nick stated.

"What's done is done," Carlo said morosely. "I'll live with it as best I can."

"There's something I'd like to know, though, Mr. Mauro, and I think you can tell me. Why did Felicia marry me? And don't tell me it was because she loved me. If you believed that you wouldn't have tried to buy me off."

"I don't know what you're talking about," Carlo said, looking away.

"I think you do."

"Felicia's reasons are her own. If you don't know them without asking her, then maybe you shouldn't know."

"So there is something."

"I didn't say that, Mr. Mondavi. I said nothing."

Nick could see he was getting the same runaround he'd gotten from Felicia. But Carlo's reaction told him he was on the right track. There was definitely something going on.

"Why can't you tell me?" Nick persisted. "What's the danger in that?"

"I can't. I just can't!" Carlo shouted. But his tone was more pleading than angry. "Look," he went on, his eyes tearing, "she's gone, as far as her mother and I are concerned. So don't torture me with questions, and don't torture Felicia. Just take her and be content. I beg you."

Nick watched him wipe his eyes with a handkerchief.

"Believe me, the less said, the better," Carlo added.

Nick heard his anxiety... and his fear. He'd noted fear in Felicia's voice, too. At the time, he'd assumed she was afraid of him, but that couldn't explain Carlo's reaction. Something else was bothering them. Something ominous.

Nick slipped from the banquette and started for the door. He was halfway across the dining room when he turned to the table. He walked back and leaned over, getting right in Carlo's face.

"It's Uncle Vinny, isn't it? That's who you and Felicia are afraid of. What did he do?"

"Just go," Carlo begged. "You can kill me if you want, but I won't say another word."

Nick could see it was hopeless. But Carlo's fear confirmed his suspicions. Vinny might have paid Felicia to marry him, but that was only part of the story. He decided to probe a little.

"Felicia claims my uncle paid her to marry me. Is that true, Mr. Mauro? Or is your daughter a liar?"

Carlo lowered his head. "No, she's not a liar. She was offered money to become your wife."

"But that's not all. What else is there? Money and what? Does it have to do with you, Carlo? Were you in the business? Were you once in my uncle's line of work?"

"No!" Carlo shouted. "Never!"

"Then what?"

"Then nothing! Take my daughter and leave. Don't ask more questions. You and your family have made me suffer enough."

Nick drew himself up. "All right," he said. "I'll see that Felicia comes by your house to say her goodbyes before we leave. So long."

Nick started for the door. Carlo stopped him.

"Felicia's a good girl, Mr. Mondavi. This hasn't been easy for anyone, her especially. Don't be hard on her. Please. It's not her fault. None of it."

Nick wondered what that meant. The words of a protective father? Or something else? But he knew there was no point in asking. So he left without another word.

DURING THE FLIGHT, Felicia was troubled by Nick's behavior. He seemed sullen and withdrawn. She wondered if it had something to do with what her father had whispered as they said goodbye. "I think Nick suspects his uncle did something besides give you money for the marriage," he'd said. "Maybe it troubles him. Be careful."

With the cabin lights low, a blanket covering her as she curled up in the big first-class seat, her father's comment kept going through her mind. Was Nick trying to figure things out? And if so, what did that mean for her?

Nick had never been rude or gruff, but she had detected hints of disdain and condescension and cynicism. Would that change if he suspected Vinny had done more than just pay her? And how might his uncle react if Nick asked him about any other involvement? Considering the promise Vinny had made her make, the whole thing might blow up in her face, and that scared her. She was torn about talking to Nick about it, but decided in the end it was too risky. She had more to lose than to gain. But one thing was certain. She'd have to be very careful.

They arrived in New York at dawn. Nick didn't own a car—he'd told her they were more trouble than they were worth. The taxi they'd ended up with was shabby. The cabby barely spoke English. His driving was unorthodox, at least to Felicia. Nick said this was the way things were in New York. It made her wonder why everybody living there hadn't wanted to move to San Francisco, like her father.

"It will seem big and dirty and unfriendly at first," her father had told her as they were saying goodbye the previous evening, "but New York has heart underneath. Even after all these years I miss it."

Queens, as viewed from the Van Wyck and Long Island expressways, did not appear very hospitable. Parts of it looked fairly run-down, in fact. Maybe it wasn't any worse than Hunter's Point in San Francisco, but it seemed alien to her nonetheless.

As she gazed out at the city, a sick, empty feeling overcame her. She wondered if it was homesickness. She hadn't traveled much. Her parents had taken her to Disneyland as a kid, and she'd gone to L.A. when she was older. She and Johnny had once gone to Las Vegas secretly. That was the closest thing to a honeymoon she'd ever had. The big travel adventure of her life was that trip to Italy with her parents when she was a teenager. This was different. She wasn't a tourist. She was coming to a new home, one Nick and the Antonellis had forced on her.

Felicia glanced at him. Nick was looking out the window. She wondered what he was thinking. About his problems? About her? Or about Gina? Maybe he'd learned that a woman who'd been coerced could never be a loving wife. She could smile, she could obey, she could allow him in her bed. But she could never love.

When they got close enough to Manhattan that the skyline became distinctive, Nick roused himself from his contemplation and pointed out some of the taller buildings. If she wanted to, she could take a tour of New York, he told her, to get a feel for the place. "At first we'll go out a lot. Since you were in the business, you should know the restaurants." It touched her that he would be that concerned about her.

In spite of everything, Felicia was curious about his house. She'd gathered that Gramercy Park had a certain cachet, but Nick said what he liked best was that it was quiet. The town house was a block from the park. He didn't have a key to the park, he told her, though with effort he probably could get one. She hadn't understood what he meant, so he explained that the park was not public, but rather owned by the residents of the surrounding buildings. It was considered a plum to have a key to Gramercy Park.

They'd talked about it on the plane, though it had taken prodding on her part. Nick told her he'd gotten the property years earlier as part of a package in a tax-free exchange for a commercial building he'd developed. "It was my first big deal," he said. "My neighbors were years older and stuffier. They had to wonder where a young kid like me got his money."

She'd listened with interest because she knew so very little about him. Much of what his aunt had told her she'd dismissed as propaganda—especially the part about Nick having nothing to do with Vincent Antonelli's business. What a disgusting euphemism that was. *Business.* Nick might not run around shooting people or breaking their legs, but she didn't believe he wasn't somehow connected with his family's criminal activities—laundering his uncle's money, if nothing else. If not that, where *did* he get his money?

If they couldn't easily discuss Nick's work, he could tell her about his home. So after they'd had their drinks and snack, she'd asked again about his town house. He explained that he'd remodeled it after Gina died, essentially gutted it. She had asked him to describe it, and he told her that in addition to the master suite there was a guest room, a small den and office, a living room, dining room and kitchen. "It isn't used much," he'd said, "but you'll change that. You'll have to buy utensils, though. I've got a few pots and pans, a spatula and a couple of wooden spoons, and a set of everyday dishes."

Felicia could see she'd have lots to do. That made her happy. She wanted the kitchen to be hers. "What's my budget?"

"Whatever you want."

They hadn't discussed decor and what, if anything, she'd be allowed to do. Felicia wasn't sure if the intent was for this to be their home together, or if she was to be a kind of housekeeper who supplied sex. Perhaps Nick himself didn't know.

They were approaching the entrance to the Queens-Midtown Tunnel when he touched her arm and pointed to the United Nations building across the river. "Remember studying that in school?"

"I made a model of it in the fifth grade," she said.

"My fifth grade class toured it. Look how much we have in common."

He was being cordial. She was glad of that, even if she didn't know how he really felt or what his intentions were. Would he tell her, or would she have to figure it out on her own? Maybe Nick was the kind of man who followed his whims. If he felt like being nice, he'd be nice. If he felt like having sex, he'd have it. Was that the kind of life she had to look forward to? she wondered. With Nick, it was hard to tell.

As they crossed under the river to midtown Manhattan, he fell silent again. Something was definitely troubling him. She fought the urge to ask what, knowing she'd just have to wait until he wanted her to know.

They came out onto East Thirty-seventh and drove west to Lexington Avenue. From there they went south fifteen or sixteen blocks to Gramercy Park. Nick had the driver circle the park so she could see the stately homes. He pointed out the Players Club and the National Arts Club. She asked if he was a member. "Owning an office tower or running for mayor or governor makes more sense for somebody like me. Two things determine what you can do in New York," he told her, "who you are and how much you've got."

"Not who you know?"

He gave her a look. "That's part of who you are, isn't it?"

"I guess you're right. Some things you can't get away from no matter how hard you try."

Neither of them had to be specific when they talked about Vincent Antonelli. Nick was as aware of that as she.

But that went out of her mind when the taxi stopped before her new home. A surge of excitement went through her. The town house wasn't so grand as those facing the park, but it was adorned with rather nice ironwork and a stately front door that was painted white. She didn't know architecture very well, but it seemed to be Georgian.

Nervous, she got out of the cab. She stared at the facade of the house as the driver unloaded their suitcases. Nick supervised, but he also watched her. Despite the hum of traffic on Broadway and Park Avenue South, it was a quiet street. She could hear the twitter of birds in the trees.

The job complete, the taxi driver held out his hand and Nick pressed some twenties into his palm. The man returned to his cab, and Nick moved to her side.

"What do you think?" he asked as the taxi drove off.

"It looks really nice," she replied, trying not to sound overeager.

"Let's go inside."

He picked up two of the larger suitcases and set them inside the gate. Felicia took a smaller one and went to the foot of the stairs. After Nick had the luggage inside the gate he joined her.

"I won't embarrass you by carrying you over the threshold," he said as they went up the steps. "But the fact is this will be your home as much as mine. I want you to know that."

She glanced at him, touched by the sentiment. It was the strongest indication yet that he intended to treat her as a real wife. "I appreciate you saying that."

"The fact is, you married me, not my uncle's money."

The comment entered her like a knife. What good he'd done with his previous statement, he'd undone with one flip remark. He seemed to realize immediately. He was in the middle of unlocking the door and stopped.

"Did that hurt you?"

She was silent, but it was answer enough.

"I'm sorry, Felicia. What I was trying to say was let's forget how we got here and start out fresh. We're married. That's the bottom line."

"Do you mean that?"

"Well, yes, I do."

"You don't sound very sure."

"It's not easy to put everything aside. What I'm telling you is that's what I want to do."

She nodded, accepting his explanation. "Me, too, I guess."

Nick pushed the door open and gestured for her to enter. She took a fortifying breath and stepped inside as he went back for the cases. The first thing she noticed was the high ceiling and the small chandelier in the entry hall. Dark hardwood floors gleamed. So did the white-painted trim. A small but attractive staircase was straight ahead. She liked it already. A lot.

The living room, to the right, was dominated by an Oriental carpet and a huge fireplace. The wing chairs and sofa were all dark green leather. The other furnishings were sparse, just a couple of occasional tables. There was one painting, an antique oil that looked to be from the colonial period.

Nick joined her. She glanced at him.

"It's very nice."

"Let's be honest. It needs a woman's touch."

"It could use softening a bit, I agree."

"I suppose you'd like to see the kitchen."

She followed him to the back of the house by way of the dining room, which was furnished with a large table with matching Queen Anne chairs. There was no buffet or sideboard, and nothing on the walls but one lithograph of a hunt scene.

They entered the kitchen. She glanced around eagerly. Nick hadn't understated the modesty of the appointments. But that was easily remedied. There was a nice stainless steel gas stove and a large matching refrigerator. The white tile counter space was limited, but workable. The cupboards were ample. She liked the double sink and the huge dishwasher, though two smaller ones would have been preferable. The hardwood floors had been extended into the kitchen—aesthetically pleasing, but not the most practical. All in all, it was more than adequate. Better than she might have hoped.

What she liked best was the tall window that looked out onto the small rear garden. It had a nice broad sill that was large enough for a small herb garden.

"That's the pantry," he said, pointing to a narrow door in the rear corner next to the outside door.

Felicia had a look. It was narrow but quite deep, affording lots of shelf space, at the moment entirely empty.

"Very nice. A pantry is a luxury."

"I'm glad you're pleased."

She let Nick know of her satisfaction with her smile.

"So, will it do?"

"It's very, very nice."

"Need anything changed?"

"I wouldn't mind a large butcher block."

"Buy it, and anything else you need. My aunt has volunteered to help. She said she'd take you to a place down on Mulberry Street in Little Italy that has everything a cook could possibly want. She said she'd call you right away, probably tomorrow."

"That would be nice."

Nick shifted uneasily. "I suppose I should show you the bedroom, too. You'll have to see it eventually."

She wasn't sure if it was sarcasm or bitterness she heard in his voice. "That's true," she said. "Unless you'd rather I sleep somewhere else."

"I think you'll find it's big enough for two."

They returned to the hall and climbed the stairs. For the first time she felt trepidation, as well as anticipation. This was to be *their* bedroom. She'd never shared a room with anyone before. It was an intimate notion. Frightening, in a way.

The master suite occupied the front half of the upstairs. It was enormous. There was a sitting room with a big fireplace, a dressing room, a huge walk-in closet, a bath with a Jacuzzi, shower and bidet. There were two basins and floor-to-ceiling mirrors.

"It's lovely," she said, looking around, having trouble thinking of it as theirs, let alone hers.

"There's another bedroom, but all that's in it is exercise equipment and a bunch of files. Gina had planned to use it as a nursery." She heard a little catch in his voice, but he moved on. "As you see, I've made room for your things in the closet," he said. "I'll get your cases so you can unpack." He hesitated. "I know you didn't get much sleep on the plane, so if you want to lie down for a nap, feel free."

He gestured toward the bed. She looked at it, her mind flashing back to their wedding night. She recalled him covering her face with her skirts, arousing her and taking her. But she also remembered his kisses and his shy, almost apologetic manner when he found her crying on the balcony.

The expression on Nick's face was not especially provocative, but it reminded her of the way he'd looked at her as he'd walked in on her in the bath the next morning. Considering he'd caught her naked, she'd half expected him to take her on the spot. But he hadn't acted on the impulse, if that was in fact what had been in his mind.

He went to the door.

"Nick," she said, stopping him.

He turned. She didn't want the uncertainty hanging over her any longer. She wanted to know his intentions. "What about you? Are you going to take a nap?"

"I deal with jet lag by staying up until bedtime, but you do as you wish." His tone wasn't cold, but neither was there warmth in it. "Is that all right?"

"Sure. Why not?"

Nick thought for a moment, then returned to where she stood. He reached out and touched her cheek affectionately. "You aren't inviting me to stay, are you?"

Felicia colored, not having seen it coming. "No, that isn't what I meant. I just . . ."

He laughed. "No, I didn't think so." He headed for the door. "Let me know if you need anything," he said. "I'm sure there's lots I overlooked."

When he was gone, she sat on the bed. She was exhausted, but that was only part of it. Nick was toying with her. She couldn't tell if his intent was to be confounding or if it was just working out that way. It seemed he was trying to make it easy for her. If so, why? More important, was it for her benefit or his?

# 10

THEY HAD DINNER that night at Nick's favorite Chinese restaurant on Mott Street in the heart of Chinatown. Just for the experience, they went down to the Lower East Side on the subway. Felicia took Nick's arm whenever an unsavory character approached. It wasn't for appearance's sake. Nick promised they'd go home in a taxi.

Living only a stone's throw from Chinatown in San Francisco, she wasn't dazzled by Mott Street, but Felicia was surprised when Nick told her it was the biggest Chinese community in the Western Hemisphere. "Yours might be older, but ours is bigger," he said.

She had taken Nick up on his offer and had had a short nap. Most of the afternoon she'd spent unpacking and wandering through the house. Nick was in his den, working at his desk and for a while watching a football game. Once she'd gone to his door to ask if he'd like coffee.

"You making yourself some?"

"I thought I would, if it's okay."

"You don't have to ask permission. The kitchen is yours."

She'd smiled.

"You don't take that as a sexist comment, do you? I didn't mean it that way," he explained.

"No, I understand. Since I'm a professional chef, the kitchen is like a studio to me. You were being generous."

He had been pleased that she understood. "Yes, that's exactly what I was thinking."

Nick, to her relief, continued to be nice. Their arrival in New York was not a spark to a Dr. Jekyll and Mr. Hyde transformation. She'd worried about that—especially after her father's warning.

As they ate, the familiar smells of Chinese food making her think of San Francisco, she wondered about Nick—who he really was. For over a week he'd been Vincent Antonelli's nephew. That was a reality she'd never exorcise from her thoughts. But apart from that, who was he? And just how important was the Antonelli connection in making Nick who he was?

More than once she'd wondered if the story Vinny had given her was a sham, and if Nick was perfectly well aware of everything that had happened. The two men might have agreed to deceive her to make it easier on Nick. And worse, what if Nick was mixed up with Vincent Antonelli's business right up to his eyebrows? They had to know a decent girl would find it easier to marry a man who wasn't involved in organized crime, especially since Vinny's own wife had left him for that very reason.

"It's early, I know," Nick said, setting his chopsticks down, "but what's your first impression of New York?"

"So far, so good."

He considered that. "No questions or problems, then?"

Felicia saw an opportunity. "On the plane you said your neighbors wondered where a young kid had gotten his money...."

"Yeah."

"So, where did you get it?"

"I got started with money my mother left for me in trust." He rubbed his jaw. "At least, that's what I thought at the time. Recently I learned the money had actually come from my uncle."

"You were surprised?"

He read her sarcasm perfectly. "You don't believe I'm legit, do you? You think I'm involved with my uncle's business."

"Your aunt called it that, too. Business."

"Look, Felicia, I'm not going to make any apologies for that. Vincent Antonelli and I have nothing to do with each other apart from the fact that he happened to be my mother's brother."

"Fine," she said. "It's none of my business, anyway. And to be honest, it's probably better if I don't know."

"Well, *I* want you to know. The fact of the matter is I'm *not* a gangster! I'm an honest businessman."

The man seated behind him looked over his shoulder.

"Whatever you say, Nick," she said under her breath.

"Whatever you say, Nick. Whatever you say. I don't want to hear that garbage, Felicia," he rejoined, sounding annoyed. "If you don't believe me, fine. There's nothing I can do about that. But there's no need to play games."

"Play games?" Her eyes flashed. "Who's playing games?"

"Save the indignation," he said. "I've told you everything. I haven't held anything back. You're the one who's been coy."

"*I've* been coy?" she said incredulously. "Vincent Antonelli's *your* uncle, not mine!"

Now Nick was the one who looked around. Only then did she realize it probably wasn't the politic thing to be blurting out in public. She lowered her voice.

"Am I wrong?" she asked.

"Do I have to remind you that you're the one who made the deal with him?" Nick said, modulating his tone. "I'm more in the dark than you."

Her mouth dropped open. "How can you say that? You must think I'm a fool!"

"This marriage thing was Vinny's idea, I grant you. But I didn't make the deal. It was basically handed to me. You, on the other hand . . ." His voice trailed off.

"I what?"

"You're . . ."

"Being paid to be your sex slave, Nick? Is that what you're trying to say?" she said, her voice rising. Several diners looked their way, but Felicia didn't care. "I can't believe you have the nerve to play the innocent in this. *I'm* the victim here, Nick Mondavi!"

"Oh? Why don't you tell me about it, then."

Felicia suddenly saw that she'd painted herself into a corner. She'd admitted to taking money to be his wife but couldn't tell him the rest of the story.

"Just explain to me how you're the victim," he said, pressing her.

She was mute.

"Well?"

"We apparently don't believe each other," she said, trying to deflect the conversation, "so there's no point arguing about it. You're going to think what you want to think, and so am I."

"Wonderful basis for a marriage." He signaled the waiter for the check.

"What difference does it make, when you come right down to it?" she asked.

It took a moment, but he finally got her point. "Of course. How silly of me to think it should."

The waiter came, and Nick settled the bill.

"Let's get out of here," he said to her, none too pleased.

They walked along Mott Street in brooding silence. Felicia wasn't sure how mad he was or whether his anger was a bad thing. Maybe she'd been too direct, too honest.

"Look," he said after a while, "I'm sorry I blew up. It wasn't a very good way to welcome you to New York."

"I didn't help matters."

He glanced at her, a smile curling his lip. "How long have we known each other? A week?"

"Not quite."

"Look at all the baggage we're already carrying. Not many newlyweds can claim that." He shook his head. "If it wasn't so pathetic, it'd be funny."

"And we can't do a damned thing about it. That's the ironic part."

"Except try to be kind to each other," he said.

There was a gentleness to his tone that struck her. "Yes, except try to be kind to each other."

Nick surprised her by putting an arm around her shoulders. "We fight, Mrs. Mondavi, but our fights don't last long. That's a hopeful sign."

"Two days of marriage and you've got it figured out?"

He laughed. "I don't hold grudges and I'm an optimist. What more could a woman want in a husband?"

"And you're modest, too," she said, rolling her tongue through her cheek.

Nick kissed her on the temple. "There may yet be hope for us, kid."

Felicia was a bit confused. "So, let me get it straight. Did I just apologize, or did you?"

He hailed a passing taxi. "Take your pick."

FELICIA SPENT an extra long time in the bathroom getting ready for bed. Nick had said he was beat and was going to hit the sack early. She'd had the nap, but she figured the thing to do was go to bed when he did. She couldn't avoid him forever, so she might as well find out what she was facing.

She chose a modest nightgown—one that didn't say she was available, but at the same time didn't say she wasn't. Nick, to her surprise, had already turned the light off on his side of the king-size bed. She slipped under the covers and reached to turn off the lamp.

Holding her breath, she eased her head onto the pillow. She listened for the sound of Nick's breathing, an indication that he might be asleep.

Two or three minutes passed with no clear sign. Then he snored softly, and she realized he *was* asleep. She gave a big sigh of relief. Of course it couldn't go on like this forever. But at least for now she had a reprieve.

She lay very still, listening to the underlying rumble of New York City by night. Being in a strange town, in a strange room, in bed with a man she hardly knew, wasn't the most pleasant situation for a woman to be in. But it could have been so much worse.

Nick was really pretty nice, if she was completely honest about it. More than anything she hated what he thought about her, his misconception about why she'd married him. She knew it bothered him, thinking she was a woman who could be bought. Maddening as it was, she also found his annoyance reassuring. At least he cared.

Her mind went back to their wedding night. He certainly hadn't made love to her like she was a stranger. To the contrary, he'd loved her as a lover would.

And he'd certainly turned her on. She blushed, thinking about it. It was raw sex, of course, with no special feelings attached . . . except for a sort of affection. Despite everything, they had a regard for each other. There had been so much going on that she hadn't been able to focus on that part. But there were definite vibrations.

She liked Nick. And a part of her—a bigger part than she was comfortable in admitting—would have liked making love with him tonight. In a way, though only at a purely sexual level, she was disappointed that nothing happened.

Nick's breathing had grown steady and had the rhythm of deep sleep. He was exhausted, not indifferent. But she felt the gnaw of regret anyway. Perfuming herself in the bath, she'd rationalized her fastidiousness as pride. But the truth was Nick called to her basic feminine instincts even if she was in his bed against her will.

She was under no illusions that this marriage meant anything. It had dramatically affected her life, of course, but it didn't define it. Nick, like the problem, would pass one day. In the interim, she'd just have to deal with him. Any positive feelings she could conjure up to make it bearable were all to the good. Women had pretended since time immemorial. Those who were fortunate halfway convinced themselves they wanted whatever fate imposed on them. That was the approach she'd decided on.

Nick stirred, his foot touching hers. It felt warm. She didn't move. He'd connected with her unconsciously. It was less threatening that way. Comforting, too. The truth was, she was feeling homesick and a little lonely. It wouldn't have been bad if he'd roused himself enough to take her into his arms and hold her without awakening. But it seemed she would have to make do with a foot.

Felicia gradually grew drowsy. As best she could recall, their feet were still touching as she drifted off. There was comfort in that. She liked Nick. She liked him quite a bit.

FELICIA SLEPT LATE. Nick was up and gone by the time she went downstairs. He'd left a note. The housekeeper, a Puerto Rican woman named Matti, would be there at nine to clean house, and he would be home for dinner. He'd call that afternoon when he had a better handle on his schedule.

Matti arrived before Felicia finished her coffee. She was a shy woman in her forties, cocoa-colored and with a perpetual grin. "Congratulations, Mrs. Mondavi," she said, shaking Felicia's hand. "Mister has needed a wife for a long time."

"Oh, he has?"

"Yes, *señora*, having different women all the time was not his style. I could see that right from the start."

"Nick had lots of women here, did he?" Felicia was curious.

"Not lots. Only when he was lonely, I think. He was too busy with his work for love. And I think he missed his wife . . . his first wife, I mean."

"Did you know Gina?"

"No, *señora*, I came to the house some years after she died. But mister talked of her often. I am surprised he didn't speak of you. You are very pretty. He must love you very much."

"We didn't know each other long before we married."

"Yes, I know this. When mister left, he said he was going to California and maybe coming home with a new wife." Matti beamed. "He made a good choice."

"Thank you."

"I hope you will have many children."

Felicia smiled. "Well, we've only been married a few days."

"I started my first baby on my wedding night," Matti said.

Felicia groaned inwardly at the thought. The phone rang.

"I'll get it, *señora*," the housekeeper said. "It could be for me. My children, they call me here often."

Felicia rinsed out her coffee cup as Matti went to get the phone. She returned in several moments. "For you, *señora*."

The call was from Maria Antonelli. "Welcome to New York and to our family," Nick's aunt said affably. "I am so happy for you both. Has it been good? Isn't Nick wonderful? I love him like a son. I was practically a mother to him, you know."

"Yes, I know Nick's fond of you."

They chatted for a minute or two, then Maria said, "If that kitchen is as bare as the last time I saw it, you need to shop. A wonderful cook must have a proper kitchen. It's a miracle you can make coffee in that one, and I already promised Nick I'd take you to get utensils and supplies. Is this afternoon too soon? I have a car and a driver. How about two?"

Matti was making the bed when Felicia went up to shower and dress. Their pillows were as far apart as possible. The center of the big bed appeared virginal. Matti was smoothing the bottom sheet. Felicia decided in the future she'd make the bed herself.

"If you want, I can always clean the downstairs first," she said. "Do the bedroom last. I'm only here three hours Monday to Friday."

"Let's try it that way," Felicia agreed.

"Do you want that I go now, *señora?*"

"No, that's fine. Finish the bed. And don't worry about the bath. I'll clean up after my shower."

Matti was quick and efficient. She was vacuuming the front room when Felicia came down. While Matti finished, Felicia spent her time in the kitchen, making lists. She was warming a can of soup for lunch when the housekeeper came to say goodbye.

"I'll see you tomorrow, *señora,*" Matti said.

"This will be a different place when you see it next," Felicia said.

"You love to cook, then?"

"Very much. Desserts, especially."

"Mister will be a very happy man, *señora*. A beautiful wife who can cook like an angel." She laughed and waved goodbye.

Felicia was pleased. Her first full day in New York was shaping up to be a good one. But she was curious how Nick would act that evening. Her first night there had been an uncertain one. They'd both given mixed signals, probably because neither of them was sure how they felt about each other or the marriage. But with each day things would get clearer. She could only hope things would get better, as well.

Maria Antonelli arrived fifteen minutes late. She greeted Felicia warmly. She was doting, talkative, grandmotherly and a bit overwhelming. She had a proud, Queen Mother air to go with her handsome face and ample figure. Her hair was still dark, but there was a large white streak running through the middle of her head. Felicia decided it gave her a regal air.

"You're even more beautiful than your picture," she told Felicia as they sat in the front room. She added cream and sugar to her coffee. "Nicky must be pleased. He was halfway in love with you even before he left New York, you know."

"He was?"

"He'd refused to go to San Francisco until he saw your picture. In fact, I had trouble getting him to come over even to discuss the matter. One look and did his tune ever change!"

Felicia chuckled. She didn't know if it was true or Maria was trying to flatter her. Vincent Antonelli had an agenda, and his estranged wife might have adopted it—or had one of her own. Felicia still didn't know the family well enough to understand their inner workings.

"Isn't Nicky a dream boat?" Maria said, sipping her coffee. "How he's stayed single all these years I'll never know."

Felicia had wondered about that herself. Matti had given a possible explanation unknowingly. "He didn't seem to lack for companionship," she said obliquely.

Maria's brows rose. "He said something about this?"

"It's obvious he knows his way around," she replied, not wanting to get the housekeeper in trouble.

"They were after him, all right, but Nicky wasn't so interested," Maria said. "He mourned Gina for years.

Frankly, you're the first woman who ever seemed to light his eyes. And from a picture, yet."

"Nick speaks of Gina with such reverence. He really must have loved her."

"Oh, he did. Nicky's such a good boy, and he was a wonderful husband, too. Who wouldn't love him? You must have discovered how good he is, Felicia."

"He can be very thoughtful."

"And elegant, don't you think? Nicky's more than handsome. It's his natural Italian charm and that Ivy League education. Class. Nicky's got class. Which is why you're perfect for him. You're the same, Felicia. I could see it in your picture, but in person it's even more. A hundred times more."

"You're sweet to say so, Mrs. Antonelli."

"Mrs. Antonelli? No, no! My driver and the maid and the shopkeepers and the lawyers call me Mrs. Antonelli, but to you I'm Maria. Please, Felicia. You're family now, after all."

Felicia watched Maria nibbling on one of the Amarettini cookies she'd found in a tin in the pantry while preparing for the visit. "Am I family enough to ask a very serious question, Maria?"

The woman had started to pick up her cup. She put it down. "Certainly, dear."

"I don't know how to put this delicately, so I'll just say it. How much of Nick's business is, well, connected to, uh . . ."

"His uncle Vinny's?"

Felicia nodded. "Yes."

Maria sighed. "You're touching a nerve, but then I guess you appreciate that."

"I didn't mean to—"

"No, no, don't apologize. I'm trying to say it's something that eats at the heart of our family. Vincent Antonelli has been the joy and curse of my life. And that has been the same for our daughters and Nicky. I can tell you honestly, Nicky and his uncle have absolutely nothing to do with each other in their work. Vinny himself insisted on it from the beginning. That was why Nicky was sent to Harvard, so he'd have a successful life without the old ways Vinny brought with him from Sicily." She paused to sip her coffee. "Because of what happened with your marriage, I can understand how you might doubt this, but it's true."

"How much do you know about Mr. Antonelli and my family?"

"I don't ask how Vinny knows people. I don't ask anything. He told me he found a nice Italian girl for Nicky, and he asked me to see that you met. I didn't know more and I didn't want to know more. I won't even ask you."

"It's just as well," Felicia said.

Maria popped another cookie in her mouth. "But why are we wasting time? Eating is the last thing I need. There is much to do. Have you made a list? A fabulous cook like you must have a thousand things you need. Wait till you see Vanducci's. There's not a shop so fine in Italy! Come," she said, getting up, "the car's out front. You'll want to make Nicky something special tonight. He told me over the phone you cook better than any woman he's ever known."

They were in the entry hall. Maria took her purse from the table. Felicia grabbed hers.

"I'm so happy Nicky's fallen in love with you," Maria said.

"Did Nick say that, Maria?"

They went out the door.

"He didn't have to," Nick's aunt replied. "It was in his voice. Heavens, you must have heard it yourself."

They went down the steps.

"A woman knows by the way a man makes love, if nothing else," Maria said under her breath. "If not during, after. After, they cannot lie."

FELICIA SPENT fifteen hundred dollars outfitting the kitchen, exclusive of the butcher block. Maria insisted on getting her something special for a wedding present, so she bought her not one, but two of the largest Cuisinart food processors made. "I have three," Maria said.

Felicia spent several hundred dollars more stocking the pantry. Some of the grocery items she took home with her. The rest were delivered later.

It took Felicia two hours to put things away and set up her kitchen. It was the first time since getting her own apartment that she had done a kitchen from scratch, and that had been minor league compared to this. Many restaurant kitchens weren't so well appointed.

The woman in the shop told her about the green market on the north side of Union Square every Wednesday, Friday and Saturday. When Felicia discovered it was six blocks from the town house, she decided to pay a visit the first chance she had. To her, fresh produce was the lifeblood of fine cuisine.

Outfitting her kitchen made her want to cook for Nick. He'd appreciated what she'd made for him so far, and his pleasure gave her pleasure. Cooking for him was something she could do without mixed feelings.

After Maria dropped her off, Felicia went to the market to get fresh poultry for her chicken Marbella, which was made with prunes and olives in an olive oil and red wine vinegar marinade. It went well with saffron rice and steamed broccoli. For dessert she planned to make her chocolate Amaretto cheesecake, a recipe she'd developed herself.

The cheesecake needed time to cool, so she decided to make it first. While it was baking, she got her herb garden started. By the time she took the cheesecake out of the oven, it was late. In her kitchen, time always seemed to fly. "It's like being an artist in his studio," her father used to say in describing the phenomenon.

Carlo wasn't creative the way Felicia was, but he loved working with food. "I'm a bricklayer, not an architect," he liked to say. He was known for serving food of a consistently high quality. That's why the restaurant had endured. If she got her dessert diner going, she'd be thrilled with half her father's success.

Just thinking about her parents made her homesick. But she didn't have time for nostalgia. She ran upstairs, had a quick shower and did her hair on top her head. She was careful with her makeup, then put on slim silk jade green pants and matching tank top.

She didn't have much time, so she hurried down to get the marinade for the chicken ready. Ideally, she'd have marinaded it the day before, but she really wanted to make this dish and so she cut corners.

Breezing into the kitchen, she came to an abrupt halt when she came face to face with Nick. His suit coat was slung over his shoulder, and he was leaning over the cheesecake. He looked at her.

"Oh!" she said with a start. "I didn't know you'd come home."

"Sicilian husbands, especially new ones, like to keep their wives guessing," he said with a smile. "What, pray tell, is this? It smells fabulous." He inhaled the fragrance.

"Chocolate Amaretto cheesecake."

"For me?"

"Well, it's not for the mailman."

He gave her a wry smile. "That's a relief."

"I knew you'd be worried."

Nick looked her over. "Lovely," he said. "Elegant."

"Thank you."

He glanced around the kitchen. "I see you've been shopping."

Her expression turned contrite. "I spent a fortune. But your aunt bought the Cuisinarts, so it's not quite as bad as it looks."

"Felicia, you're worth every penny. The way you cook . . ."

"It's a new kitchen, so there may be some slips," she said.

Nick gave her another admiring glance, a lengthy one. "I'm a new husband. What do I know?"

"You'll be able to tell if a sauce is burned."

He sauntered toward her, a partly naughty, partly playful expression on his face. He moved right into her space, making no attempt to hide his salacious smile. "Sweetheart, you've got all the slack you need. I'm pretty easygoing when it comes to the fairer sex."

"So I hear."

His brows rose. "Don't tell me Aunt Maria's been talking."

"Oh, she had nothing but praise for you, Nick. I learned that you walk on water, among other things. I was thinking of Matti."

"Ah. She can be too candid for her own good," he said, only slightly embarrassed. "I'd better have a word with her."

"Don't you dare! I've got a good relationship with her, and I don't want you messing it up. Accept the fact you don't have any more secrets . . . at least in this house. At work, I don't know."

"For a beginner, you're pretty clever at this wife business," he said, tweaking her chin.

His proximity and his touch made her heart skip a few beats. He was being more seductive than she'd have expected. She wondered if her conciliatory signal had been too strong.

"So, how was it being back in your office?" she asked.

He gave her a dark look.

"I'm not suppose to ask?"

Nick sighed. "I'm not one who likes to bring his problems home from the office."

"Forget I asked, then. I was just trying to be polite."

She started to turn away, but Nick grabbed her by the waist, holding her firm. "I wasn't being critical, Felicia. I was explaining my philosophy."

"That's okay, Nick. Whatever you want is fine."

She tried again to move, but he still wouldn't let her. "You might as well know what happened, because you're affected. I had a call from my immigration lawyer, Helen. Not good news. There've been a couple of cases in the past month or so that are bad precedents for our side. The INS was allowed even more discretion in their interpretation of the immigration laws. The long and the short of it is, I'm probably in for the fight of my life."

"Nick, I'm sorry."

"The worst part is that the bastards have me twisting in the wind. There's no telling when they'll come down on me. I almost wish they'd serve me so I can get it over with."

On an impulse Felicia put her arms around him, giving him a hug. "Are you scared, Nick?"

He hugged her back. "It's no fun thinking they could throw me out of the only country that's ever been home to me."

Her heart went out to him, but when he squeezed her tightly and inhaled her scent, she realized that maybe her compassion had carried her a little too far.

"It's a comfort knowing you're at my side though, Felicia," he murmured in her ear.

She pulled away, confirming there was a bemused smile on his lips. She gave him a scornful look. "I'm practicing for the INS, Nick. That's all."

She tried to move once again, but Nick wouldn't let her escape. He pulled her even closer. "Don't go. I meant that sincerely."

"Yeah, sure."

"There's not a woman in the world I'd rather have in my corner. Honest."

"Save it for the INS," she said dryly.

He took her chin in his hand and kissed her on the mouth, catching her by surprise. She didn't resist, but she didn't exactly embrace him, either. Afterward he gave her a self-satisfied grin and tapped her on the end of the nose with his finger. "I'll save the bull for the government, but that kiss was for your benefit, kid."

This time she managed to make good her escape, though more to hide the color in her cheeks than to protest his affection. She went to the refrigerator and looked inside, though she had no particular reason. Nick moved to the counter nearby, leaning on it as he watched her. She glanced at him.

"What are you doing, Nick?"

"Watching you."

"What for?"

He shrugged. "I don't know, maybe I want to see a brilliant chef at work."

"You're so full of it."

"It appears that the first thing to do is study what's in the refrigerator."

Felicia flushed, closing the door. She faced him, putting her hands on her hips. "You must have something better to do, Mr. Mondavi, than harass me."

"Mmm. I love your fire, sweetheart."

"Shut up, Nick."

He threw back his head and laughed. "Okay, I'll be good. How long before dinner?"

She glanced at the clock. "It's only five. Dinner won't be for two hours or so. I haven't even started the chicken, and it's best served at room temperature."

"Could there be a before-dinner bottle of wine in our future, then?"

"Not if you want a perfect meal."

"I'd settle for semiperfect."

"That's terribly open-minded of you."

"Not even one glass?"

"Just before dinner, but not while I'm cooking."

"Okay, we'll do it your way," he said. "Maybe I'll have a workout on my rowing machine before I get cleaned up, then." He headed for the door. "Save me some pots to scrub," he said over his shoulder.

"You can be in charge of garbage," she called after him. "And windows. I don't do windows."

Nick, who'd gone out the door, stuck his head back in. "You're a stern taskmaster," he said.

"New wives have to get new husbands off on the right foot," she quipped. "Otherwise they get complacent."

"I appreciate the warning."

"The main thing is that we understand each other," she said.

"I'm learning."

"To be honest, Nick, I expected more of a fight from you."

"New husbands are gullible, sweetheart. Besides, I'm taking the long view." He winked and left for his workout and shower.

# 11

NICK CARRIED the silverware into the dining room and laid it where Felicia had put the place mats, at opposite ends of the long table. Feeling something more was needed, he got the candlestick from the mantel in the living room. He put it in the middle of the table, lit it and stepped back to enjoy the effect. Just then, Felicia entered with a trivet, the china and wineglasses.

"What do you think?" he asked, as she noticed the candle.

"It's nice," she said, putting the trivet near her place.

"Nice, eh?" He watched the way her long, graceful fingers moved as she set the table. And there was something especially sensual about her bare arms and shoulders in the light of the wobbling flame. "Think it's too romantic?"

"If it pleases you, it's fine with me."

"That the best reaction I can get out of you?"

She gave him a stern look, placing her hands on her hips. "Am I being too accommodating, or not enough?"

He shrugged. "How do you feel?"

"Well, I'm not an actress, Nick. Or at least not a very good one."

"Then I'm happy that you're happy that I'm happy."

She rolled her eyes and headed for the kitchen. "Did I mention your aunt said you were spoiled?" she said as she disappeared from sight.

"Did she really? My dear aunt Maria?"

He followed her, catching a glimpse of her graceful stride before she disappeared again. He entered the kitchen. Felicia was patting the side of the roasting pan to make sure it was as cool as she wanted it.

"What makes you feel I'm spoiled?" he said, leaning on the counter across from her. He stared at the long, thin neck and the smooth lines of her jaw, her flawless skin and the loose strands of hair at her pretty ears. Standing close to her, he again caught the richness of her womanly scent. It aroused him.

She glanced at him. He peered into her eyes, giving her a quizzical look. She tried to affect a stern expression, but couldn't.

"I don't know why you feign innocence, Nick Mondavi. You're about as innocent as Donald Trump."

"Yeah, the only difference between Donald and me is a few hundred million."

"A few hundred million what?"

He chuckled. "Yen, lira, pesetas. At a certain point it hardly matters whether you're talking pennies or dollars."

"I think you're being modest," she told him.

"The Donald and I have a lot in common, actually. We both own buildings in Manhattan and we both have beautiful wives."

"But you married for different reasons."

"I wouldn't trade places with him," Nick said. "Marla's probably not half the cook you are."

"You haven't eaten yet."

She handed him bowls of rice and broccoli. He stood there, watching as she transferred the chicken from the copper roasting pan to a new platter that was deep enough to hold the juices. When Felicia started for the dining room, he followed her, thinking of her shapely legs under the soft, clingy fabric of her pants.

He had delightful recollections of those legs. Though their wedding night had been tarnished by the unfortunate circumstances of their marriage, he had pleasant memories of the physical woman he'd taken as his wife. Besides which, tonight Felicia seemed . . . different. As if she'd changed. In his mind, at least, she was becoming more the woman his aunt had found for him and less the woman his uncle had bought.

In fact, he tried not to think of how she'd come to him. Maybe his aunt's call that afternoon had affected his thinking as much as anything that had happened. "Nicky, she's a dream! The perfect wife. I couldn't have done better for you if I'd talked to every girl in New York. You must be so happy. How could you not love her? Nicky, I'm so pleased! I love her for you!"

And he had to admit, Felicia *had* seemed different when he'd gotten home. The new impression was probably due to her seeming change of attitude more than anything his aunt had said. Felicia had become . . . it was hard to say what. More engaging, maybe more confident and relaxed. She had a newfound charm, a sparkle he hadn't seen before.

Was it an acceptance of the situation, or was it that she was beginning to trust him? He had to admit she was in a tough situation. And he hadn't exactly made it easy for her. That was something he was ashamed of. But he was determined to make it up to her. Especially now, when she was being so sweet. Her change of heart couldn't have come at a better time. The call from his lawyer that afternoon had put him in a gloomy mood. Felicia, lovely Felicia, was proving to be the perfect antidote, however.

There was still half a bottle of wine left from their before-dinner drink. He filled her glass while she dished the chicken Marbella onto his plate.

"Want some sauce on your rice?" she asked.

"Please."

She gave him lots of olives, prunes and capers. Nick took his plate to his end of the table and waited as Felicia served herself. She was a delight to watch.

"Why are you looking at me that way, Nick?" she asked.

"Am I looking at you?"

"You haven't touched your dinner."

"Oh," he said, picking up his fork. He took a couple of hasty bites. "Mmm. Fabulous. Absolutely fantastic!"

She gave him a bemused smile. "I could have given you a plate of dog food and you'd have said the same thing."

"Food? Food? I was talking about the cook."

"Oh, quit teasing, Nick."

"It's not the wine," he said. "I'm not drunk. I think it's those silk pants."

She gave him another challenging look. "Well, thank your uncle, not me. It was his money that bought them."

He sighed with annoyance. "You could have gone all evening without saying that."

"Well, it's true."

He put down his fork. "Look, let's make a deal. Uncle Vinny will not be mentioned in this house again. All right?"

"It's your home."

Nick wanted to say, "No, damn it, it's your home, too," but that wasn't really true. Yet. But they'd made amazing strides. Twenty-four hours ago they were recovering from a rocky wedding night, sleeping in the same bed but behaving like strangers. But for some reason, tonight he felt married to her. It was a happy thought.

"Am I wrong?" she asked.

"What?"

"You seemed so ponderous just now."

"Ponderous?"

"Hello, Nick. Welcome to the dinner party. I hope I'm not boring you already. This is only our first dinner at home."

He smiled, embarrassed. "Oh, sorry. I was thinking."

"That's what I gathered."

"About you, Felicia."

"Oh?"

"Pleasantly."

She drank some wine. "I'm afraid to ask more."

"A wife's entitled to know what a husband thinks about her."

"Maybe we should change the subject," she said.

Nick took a bite of chicken, concentrating on the wonderful flavor. The woman could cook. "This truly is fabulous, by the way. Both the chef and the cuisine are exceptional."

He thought he could detect a blush, even in the dim light.

They ate in a companionable silence, glancing at each other past the flickering candle. Outside it was nearly dark, so the flame was the only light they had. Felicia was lovely. The simplicity of her outfit, and the way she had her hair piled on her head, made her seem almost maidenlike. His heart welled with affection, tempered only by a lingering twinge of regret.

FELICIA WASN'T SURE what to make of Nick's behavior. He was as sweet as his aunt had said. Could it be possible this was the real Nick Mondavi, instead of the man she thought she'd married? Of course, even that Nick hadn't been all bad, but this one was a little too good to be true.

"Nick," she asked, "are you really worried about being deported?"

"Helen said the INS will be investigating me thoroughly with a hearing to follow. In other words, the heat's definitely on."

"Then you weren't exaggerating."

"Nope. It appears the government and I are going to the mat. Which means you will come in very handy."

"I'm certainly glad to hear that."

He took a bite, watching her as he chewed. "Want in on a secret?"

"What?"

"I wouldn't have regretted marrying you even if Helen had told me the INS decided to drop the case and I was home free."

Felicia hadn't expected to hear that, at least not quite so directly. She wondered if he really meant it, or if it was just part of the seduction that seemed to be in progress. "Really?"

"You're surprised?"

"I didn't know that's where we were . . . or I should say that's where *you* were."

"You don't like the fact that I might actually have feelings for you?"

"It's better than if you hated me, I guess."

"Hey," he said with mock annoyance, "why are you playing hard to get?"

"Is that what I'm doing? I didn't realize. I'm sorry. What should I have said?"

Nick smiled, sipping his wine. He seemed to think she was playing games with him, but she wasn't. She was half serious. Maybe entirely serious. Why was he romancing her? What did he really want?

"You might have said you were pleased," he said, looking at her over the rim of his glass.

"I'm pleased, Nick."

He chuckled.

She *was* glad, and she hoped what he said was true. There was nothing in their agreement that said they had to love each other, or even act like they did. So his comment was a kindness, even if he had ulterior motives.

"You don't believe me, do you?" he asked.

"I believe you."

He contemplated her, looking very sexy, very seductive. She assumed he had romance in mind. Then a thought occurred to her. Maybe the call from his lawyer had put the fear of God into him. Maybe he was feeling insecure and needed the assurance she'd be sticking by him. After all, if he *was* deported she wouldn't be greatly inconvenienced. To the contrary, it would work to her advantage, because she'd be free. So maybe he wanted more than just his uncle's money to ensure her loyalty. Maybe he'd decided adding some love to the mix wouldn't hurt.

"Felicia, what are you thinking?"

"Huh?"

"You looked like you were having a very serious conversation with yourself just now."

"Oh, did I? I guess I was."

"Care to share?"

"You've forgotten, Nick," she said, picking up her glass, "my thoughts are for me alone."

"You aren't making it easy for me, are you?"

"Making what easy?"

"Normalizing our relationship," he said.

"What do you mean, normalizing?"

"The baggage we've brought to the marriage. I'd like to throw it overboard. I don't have to spell it out, do I?"

"No. I understand."

Nick slipped into a contemplative silence. Felicia could see he was frustrated. But he had no idea of the predicament she was in. Sure, if money was all that was involved, he might wonder about her loyalty. But there was a lot more between her and Vincent Antonelli than their business deal. Nick had to know that if she lost her enthusiasm for the marriage Vinny would make her pay dearly. So it had to be something else. Then it occurred to her. Maybe Nick wanted more than just a sporting effort from her. Maybe he wanted to be sure she'd do anything and everything in her power to save him. Maybe what he wanted was the dedication of a loving wife.

"But you're not sure," Nick said.

She thought for a moment, then decided to meet the issue head-on. "What if despite our best efforts you get deported anyway?"

"You're asking if I'll have the same enthusiasm for you when you're no longer in a position to make a difference."

"I suppose so."

"A fair question," he said. "The answer is my feelings for you have nothing to do with the case, the call I received this afternoon."

"I see."

"But that will be a tough one to prove, won't it?"

"I won't know until and unless you *are* deported," she said.

"Catch-22."

Felicia toyed with her fork, feeling doubt because everything was so murky. Nick had no idea what her real motives for marrying him were, and she couldn't trust his feelings for her because he badly needed a loving wife and was therefore at her mercy.

"I know what you're thinking," he said. "So let me be brutally frank. Helen told me the worst thing is how unpredictable these cases can be. They often turn on intangibles, emotional issues like children, family, whatever plucks the heartstrings. I do need you, Felicia, but I want you to know you're not just an ornament in a legal brief. What happens when we're talking to the INS and in court is one thing. What happens here in our home is another."

It was uncanny how he'd read her mind. "Being an ornament is my job, Nick. It's what I signed on to do, and it's why you married me."

"Just because we started with that in mind doesn't mean we're stuck with it. People enter relationships with one notion and end up somewhere else all the time. This is no different."

"Perhaps."

"Tell me the truth. Are you averse to letting nature take its course?"

She knew what nature he had in mind—the nature normally played out in the bedroom. "Whatever works, Nick," she said.

"Do you mean that, or is it Uncle Vinny's money talking?"

A dark feeling rose in her. "I thought we weren't going to talk about him anymore."

"I'm sorry. I take that back."

"But to answer your question, I'll try to keep an open mind. I'm not being coy. You've got to understand women don't switch gears as quickly as men. I like you, Nick. I'll admit that. But don't expect me to become someone else overnight."

"Fair enough," he said, digging into his meal. "I can't ask for more than that."

They ate for a while. Nick helped himself to seconds, which pleased her.

"Tell me more about the dessert restaurant you want," he said. "Is it something you'd consider doing sooner rather than later?"

"Oh, that's just a dream. Something for the future."

"Why not do it now? You'll be bored soon, if you aren't already."

Felicia didn't expect that. "You wouldn't mind?"

"I'd say it's your decision. You have resources, don't you?"

She assumed he was referring to the money Vincent Antonelli had promised her. She hadn't been told when she'd be getting the money—not that she'd had a lot of time to worry about it with all that had been happening—but it had crossed her mind that Vinny might stiff her. Of course, that was the last thing she'd discuss with Nick.

"Yes, I have resources," she said, "but . . ."

"But what? You have the expertise to develop and run the place, I assume. I could help you with the real estate part of the deal, if that's what concerns you."

"Would you?"

"Aren't husbands supposed to help their wives?" There was a trace of irony in his tone, but maybe some wistfulness, as well.

"It's something to think about, Nick."

He gave her a very penetrating look. "I told you I'm taking the long view, and I meant it."

His words warmed her, maybe because deep down it was what she wanted to hear. If she was giving Nick a bad time, if she was dragging her feet, it was because she was afraid. She could see that now. But even if he meant every word, even if he was beginning to fall in love with her, how could she trust it would last? There were so many things still in the way—Nick's case, the truth about Vinny and her father, the money. Could they really pretend none of that existed?

"So, are you ready for cheesecake?" she asked when he pushed back his plate.

"I've been thinking of it longingly, as a matter of fact. But I've got a suggestion. How about a little stroll around the neighborhood to clear the palate first?"

She chuckled. "Right, New York air is so much better than sherbet."

"Hey, Miss Smarty Pants, this is my neighborhood we're talking about. At least we can go outside this time of year without getting frostbite from your San Francisco fog. Anyway, it was a wonderful day. Cooler than usual. I bet it's still pleasant out."

"Yes, sir."

Nick wagged a finger at her. She laughed.

"You might want a sweater, just in case."

"Okay," she said, getting up. She picked up her plate and silver. "I'll just clear the table first."

He got up, too. Felicia went to his end of the table for his dishes. Nick handed them to her, then let his hand move lightly over her waist.

"While we're walking I'll fantasize about that cheesecake. Expectation makes something desired all the sweeter when you finally get it, you know."

Nick was standing very close to her. She was trapped between him and the table, a plate in each hand. He leaned toward her, a bemused smile on his face.

"What delicious joy to have a woman right where you want her," he said in a low, husky voice.

Closing his eyes, he puckered his lips and leaned still closer. Felicia ducked under his arm and made her escape.

"Hey," he called after her in protest, "not fair."

"A woman who's worked her whole life in a restaurant knows how to handle drunks and louts," she said, leaving the room.

Nick came along behind her. "Which are you accusing me of being?"

"Take your pick," she teased. She put the dishes down next to the sink. He came up behind her. She darted past him again.

"Are you playing hard to get, Mrs. Mondavi?" he protested.

"No, I'm going to get my sweater. I believe that's what you instructed me to do, oh lord and master."

"Wonderful trait in a woman," he shouted after her. "Obedience."

Felicia ran up the stairs, laughing all the way.

SHE LOOKED at the houses of their neighbors as they strolled, marveling that she was actually here in New York.

And married! "Bet my father would find it ironic that I'm living in a neighborhood like this."

"Why do you say that? Your parents' place in San Francisco is nice, very nice, in fact."

"Yes, but Pops told me about the neighborhood where he grew up in Brooklyn. It was very humble compared to this."

"Do you still have relatives in New York?"

"Yes, but I don't know any of them."

"Why's that?"

Felicia couldn't tell if the question was innocent or if he was leading her into a trap, because she still wasn't absolutely sure what Nick knew or didn't know. Her father had warned her to be careful. In the end, she supposed time would tell.

"When Pops left Brooklyn, he lost contact with his family. We never came back," she explained, watching to see his reaction.

"Doesn't sound like a good Italian family to me."

"My father was independent," she said, hoping he'd let the matter drop.

"Maybe you'd like to see if you can find some cousins or something," he suggested, not letting go. "It might be fun."

She shook her head. "No, I don't think so."

"I think you're as independent as your father, Felicia."

"I'll take that as a compliment."

Nick put his arm around her shoulder as they went under a streetlight. They walked for a while in silence. She decided he probably didn't have any ulterior motives after all. That came as a relief.

The night air was pleasant. It was good to get out, but she wondered about his growing affection—whether he was signaling what he had in mind for later in the evening. Yet in a way, if she was honest, the idea had more than a modicum of appeal. She had enjoyed making love with Nick. Sure, she'd been scared and too emotional to get everything she could out of it. But there was no denying that the man turned her on.

Soon they came to the park, safe behind the high wrought-iron fence. It probably wasn't a place to be at night, but by day it would be a tranquil setting amid the chaos of urban life, an ideal place of refuge in a big city like New York.

"Nice park, isn't it?" Nick said, reading her thoughts.

"It does seem peaceful."

"Would you come during the day if you had a key?"

"Probably. Once I've settled in, I'll have more time on my hands."

Nick was thoughtful as they continued around the park. "Monday, I'm going to talk to this fellow I know who leases out restaurant locations," he said. "It'd be a good idea if I familiarize myself with the market."

"What are we talking about now?"

"Your dessert diner. Just Desserts."

She felt a little shiver of pleasure. "Saying the name makes it seem so real," she said with enthusiasm. "Are you serious about helping me find a location?"

"Absolutely. I've been thinking maybe we could spend some time checking out different parts of town. Location is everything, you know."

Felicia couldn't help but be excited. "It's something I've wanted for so long, but I was never quite sure that it would be more than a dream. Having it has always been way off in the future."

"The future is now, my dear." He slipped his arm around her waist. "I'll be your best customer. I'll come in every day." He turned to her. "Have you worked out the menu?"

She grinned. "You bet. I've been thinking about it for years. There'll be chocolate mousse—"

"The one you made me the first night I came to your apartment?"

"Yes. And fruit tarts, Italian ices and biscotti, brownies and various cakes. Maybe a homemade ice cream every once in a while."

"And what about your cheesecake? I was planning on having a slice of that every day—" he gave her a squeeze "—unless, of course, I got all I wanted at home."

"Why do I get the feeling we're not talking about food?" she said.

Nick leaned over and kissed her behind the ear. "Could be because we've got something else on our minds."

*We?* she thought. But then she had to smile. Nick did have her wanting to forget who they really were and why she was there. He had her starting to take the long view herself.

They went to the town house and had the chocolate Amaretto cheesecake in the front room. Nick brought the candle from the dining room and put on some music. He was so smooth Felicia couldn't help wondering if Matti hadn't understated his prowess with the ladies.

But the cheesecake did distract him for a few minutes. "I'm going to run out of superlatives," he said. "This is good enough to make a grown man cry."

"If you say you like it, that's good enough, Nick," she said with a laugh.

"You made this entirely from scratch?"

"Is the Pope Catholic?"

"Foolish question."

They were seated side by side on the leather sofa. Nick moved closer, resting his elbow on the cushion behind them.

"So tell me, how do you make this delightful dish?" He touched her face with the tip of his finger and ran it along her jaw.

Felicia swallowed hard. "Well . . . the key is the Amaretti cookies . . . in the crust. It's . . . the same principle as using . . . graham crackers. . . ."

He leaned close so that his mouth was near her ear. She could feel his warm breath on her neck.

"Nick," she protested, "what are you doing?"

"I got distracted. You smell good. Sorry, go on."

"And what makes the filling distinctive is ... the liqueur ... the Amaretto."

He was fiddling with her earlobe, distracting her. She gave an exasperated sigh and looked him in the eye.

"Nick."

He touched his finger to her lip. "Don't chastise me," he said softly. "You're every bit as distracting as your cheesecake is delicious. Both irresistible." He leaned closer and kissed the corner of her mouth. Lightly. Briefly. Delicately.

The gesture sent a shiver through her body. She'd been resisting him, but she didn't know why. Ever since she'd gotten in bed the night before and found him asleep, she'd been looking forward to the next time they'd be together. The truth was, she wanted his affection. She wanted to be with him.

He lightly nuzzled her ear. Her heart beat nicely.

"Is this what you meant by taking the long view?" she cooed.

"It's a start." He gently pressed his soft lips against her ear. "To be honest, I've been thinking about this all day."

"It crossed my mind a time or two, as well."

"That's good to hear."

His breath on her skin sent shivers up her spine. He kissed the back of her neck. She didn't move, but she was getting very excited. The image of him throwing her wedding dress up over her face flashed through her mind, and she pressed her knees together in response to the warm feeling inside her.

"Do you like to dance?" he asked, drawing his finger down the side of her bare neck.

"Dance?"

"We're married," he said, "and we've never danced together. That's got to be a violation of one law or another."

She laughed. "There are a lot of things we've never done, Nick."

"There's only one way to remedy that. We've got to tackle them one at a time."

He got up and, taking her hand, pulled her to her feet. "Let's find out if Fred and Ginger have any competition."

Nick led her to the corner, off the Oriental carpet. There was a ballad playing on the stereo, a tune with lots of piano and mellow sax. Nick folded her into his embrace as if he'd done it a thousand times.

They fit together nicely. Some bodies worked together better than others. Johnny Fano had been thin and shorter than Nick. She hadn't recalled not feeling comfortable in his arms. In fact, to the best of her recollection it had been good. But it wasn't like this.

Nick turned his face into her hair and inhaled deeply, tightening his grip on her waist. This was a man who knew how to turn a woman on, she realized.

"If I ask you something, will you tell the truth?" she said.

He pulled his head back so he could see her. "I suppose that depends. What's the question?"

"Is this your usual routine when you bring women here? Do you always start with candlelight and dancing?"

"Is that curiosity or insecurity I'm hearing?"

"Curiosity."

"Okay. This has happened before—a variation—but it's not habitual. You're the first wife I've done it with, as a matter of fact."

"Amusing," she said with a laugh. "But I guess it does put me in a rarefied group."

Nick stopped dancing. He took her hands and looked straight into her eyes. "I don't regard you as just another date. And I'm not just trying to make the best of the situation. I'm very, very attracted to you. And the fact that you're my wife makes it all the sweeter."

"You don't have to say that."

"I know I don't. But you wanted the truth. Do you know what was the first thing I thought when I woke up this morning?"

She shook her head.

"I looked over at you and saw you sleeping peacefully beside me and I thought I'd died and gone to heaven. I didn't know how I could be so lucky. It was all I could do to keep from waking you up and making love to you."

The tune ended, and the CD player changed disks. Nick held her hands as they stood facing each other.

"That's a very nice thing to say."

"I consider myself incredibly lucky that of all the women they could have found for me, the one I got was you."

She gazed into his eyes, seeing emotion that seemed so genuine. "I feel the same," she said, her eyes shimmering.

Nick took her face in his hands and kissed her. It was a deep and loving kiss, and her immediate response was to melt into his embrace. She accepted his affection, returning it in kind, the anxiety she'd felt swept away by a rush of excitement. She kissed him back, the tingly feeling that had been coursing through her body growing more intense. He crushed her against his chest and kissed her again.

Fire rushed through her, and she began to pulse. Nick ran his hands under her tank top and unfastened her bra. He teased her nipples with his thumbs and pressed her pelvis against his. Their kiss became desperate and the next thing she knew he was taking off her top and nuzzling her breasts.

She held his head against her chest, but released the pressure enough so that he could swirl his tongue around her nipples. Then he dropped to his knees, pulling down her silk pants. When she stepped out of them and kicked off her shoes, she had on nothing but bikini panties. Nick pressed his face against them, his warm breath penetrating the sheer fabric, arousing her still more.

"Oh," she moaned, "oh, Nick."

He kissed her mound through the lace. Her head rolled back as the tingling turned into a throb. He pulled her panties down and began kissing her the way she wanted, the feathery touch of his tongue sending a jolt through her. It was so strong her knees buckled.

Before she knew it, she was on the Oriental carpet and Nick was taking off his clothes. She wanted him so desperately and her excitement was so great that her breath was coming in jerks. Her legs were trembling, and every hair on her body was standing on end.

He was erect, his shaft curving gently upward. As he moved over her, she reached out and touched his penis. She wanted him in her.

But he did not take her immediately. First he kissed her breasts, making her nipples so hard they hurt. Then he drew his tongue over her abdomen. As he neared her mound, she parted her legs. He kissed her intimately again, and she cried out, lifting against him, nearly losing her mind right then and there.

She'd never been so excited before. She was breathing hard, as though she'd just run up a flight of stairs. "Oh, God," she moaned breathlessly. "Oh, God."

This was not her husband. It was not even Nick Mondavi. Now, at this moment, he was just her lover, the man she wanted above all else.

His tongue found her nub. The sensation was electric. She felt another hot rush of liquid between her legs. The pleasure was so intense it was almost painful. She had to stop him.

"I want you inside me now. Please," she begged.

He moved between her legs and entered her.

Nick began thrusting at once. Felicia gasped, holding him as the throbbing grew more and more intense. Until she couldn't hold back any longer.

They came together. Afterward, Nick melted into her arms. She embraced him as lover, not conqueror. She wasn't sure what it felt like to be a wife, but she hoped it was much more like this than the way she'd felt on their wedding night. This was ecstasy.

After a minute or so Nick began to recover. He kissed her neck, then moved off her. Lying beside her on his back, he took her hand and sighed. "I hope you realize how special that was," he murmured softly and with reverence.

"To you?"

"Yes, and I hope to you."

She rolled onto her side and took his face in her hand. "It was very special, Nick. Nobody has ever made love to me that way before. It was wonderful."

He kissed her lips and put his arm around her, gathering her close. "It's only the beginning, my love," he whispered. "Only the beginning."

"Do you really think so?"

He caressed her face, smiling. "You think I was faking that?"

"Well, I know you were excited."

"Sweetheart, that's not what I'm talking about."

She lay with her head on his shoulder. The floor was hard, but she didn't mind. She'd been so swept up in their lovemaking they could have been anywhere.

"*You* weren't acting, were you, Felicia?"

"No," she said, kissing his chin. "It wasn't an act."

This time there was no need to lie. To him. Or to herself. Something special *had* happened. Felicia realized she was falling in love.

# 12

OVER THE NEXT FEW DAYS their lives settled into a pattern. Neither of them was eager to let go of what they'd found their second night in New York. They discussed many things when they were together—her plans for the house, his problems with the INS, her dessert diner—but they didn't talk about the events that had brought them together.

Felicia didn't know if he was afraid the bubble might burst, or if he had decided it didn't matter what induced her to marry him. Either way, she made herself forget everything when she was in Nick's arms, loving him as though Vinny didn't exist.

Still, it wasn't as if they had nothing to worry about. Nick spent two afternoons with his immigration lawyer, preparing his case. The second time Felicia went with him so the attorney could meet her.

Helen Stevens was a mannerly woman of forty-five. She was professional, no-nonsense. Her offices were in a modest suite in one of the lesser buildings on Madison Avenue in midtown.

"Mrs. Mondavi," she said, at the start of their interview, "the INS won't mince words with you, so I won't either. It's best if you get used to it."

"I understand."

"Why did you marry your husband?" Helen asked. "We might as well begin at the heart of the matter."

Felicia glanced at Nick. "At first because he seemed like an excellent prospect. His aunt introduced us. Nick was eager to marry me, and I agreed. But I soon came to care for him very much."

"Do you live as husband and wife in the usual sense of the term?"

"You're asking if we have sexual relations."

Helen Stevens shrugged.

"Yes. We care for each other just like any other married couple."

"Do you plan to have children?"

"I'm willing. That is, I'm certainly not against it."

The lawyer leaned back in her chair, studying her. "I like your manner, Mrs. Mondavi. Your answers are measured. They have the sound of someone wanting to be accurate. If you had claimed you passionately loved your husband and agreed to marry him after only a few days for love . . . Well, frankly I wouldn't have believed you, and probably no one else would, either."

"I was being honest," Felicia said, drawing a smile from Nick.

"Our feelings for each other are entirely mutual," Nick said to the lawyer.

The woman nodded. She didn't smile, but came close. "You've made a good match, let me say that, Mr. Mondavi. The INS could hardly expect more."

After they'd finished with the attorney, Nick put Felicia in a cab, saying he had some things to do at his office but he'd try to get home early. "Would you like to go out to dinner tonight?" he asked, peering in the taxi.

"I've got shrimp marinating. Why don't we go out tomorrow instead?"

"I guess a nice quiet evening at home wouldn't be bad." He gave her a wink. "Especially with a beautiful, loving wife."

"Don't get too full of yourself, Mr. Mondavi."

Nick laughed and closed the door of the taxi. The driver went to Park Avenue and turned south. Felicia looked out the window at the city. It was a beautiful, unseasonably warm day. Nick had told her autumn would come rushing in in a few months, so while the good weather lasted, they should enjoy it. "A drive up the Hudson to see the fall colors might be nice."

She couldn't think about Nick without being cheered, though she was plagued by a gnawing realization that they were ignoring certain realities. Several times over the past few days she had wanted to talk about Vinny, tell Nick the truth once and for all. The burden was difficult to live with, besides which she didn't want to keep the secret forever—not considering how well they were getting along. But Nick had been adamant that they wouldn't talk about his uncle. And besides, she sensed that telling Nick before his legal problems were settled wouldn't be a good idea. He had enough on his plate.

The taxi pulled up in front of the town house, and Felicia paid the driver and jumped out. She was hot and sticky, so the first thing she did was have a shower and change into a T-shirt and shorts. Then she went to the kitchen. She'd never made Nick her chocolate cream cheese brownies, which would go well with the casual meal she had planned.

She got out the ingredients and was in the middle of melting the chocolate when the doorbell rang. Felicia padded to the door in her bare feet and peered through the peephole. It was Louie. The sight of the man sent her heart pounding. Anybody connected with Vincent Antonelli was bad news.

For a moment she considered ignoring him. Then she realized she couldn't avoid him forever. She opened the door.

Louie greeted her with a grin. He glanced at her bare legs, then the shorts and T-shirt. Felicia hadn't bothered to put on a bra. Until she saw Louie's leer, she'd forgotten. She crossed her arms over her breasts.

"Afternoon, Mrs. Mondavi," he said. "Hope I didn't catch you at a bad time," he added with a chuckle.

"I was baking."

He took a whiff of the air. "Bread?"

"No, brownies. What do you want?" she demanded.

He looked out at the street. "I've got something for you from the gentleman who called on you in 'Frisco. But it's kind of public here. Mind if I come in?"

Felicia knew she had no choice. She admitted him. Louie glanced at the chandelier. "Nice place Nicky's got here. Hope you're enjoying it."

"Yes, it's a very nice house."

"The marriage working out okay?"

She didn't like the questions, but she knew perfectly well where they were coming from.

"I'm very happy," she said evenly but without enthusiasm.

"That's good. Real good."

"You didn't come here to ask about my marriage," she said.

"Actually I did, Mrs. Mondavi. Word is, things are going pretty good between you and Nicky."

"We're getting along okay."

"Word is it's more than okay," he said, lifting his brow.

Felicia wondered what that meant. Did Vinny Antonelli have their bedroom bugged? Or did Nick have to send in reports to his uncle? No, he wouldn't do that, even if he was asked. It had to be Maria.

"Well, you can tell Mr. Antonelli things are just fine between Nick and me. He doesn't have to worry."

"That's good, real good. He'll be glad. But, you see, it also creates a problem."

Felicia didn't know what he meant. "What kind of a problem?"

"Well, Vinny was hoping Nicky would like you, that you'd make him happy and all that. But Vinny's a little worried about the future."

"Why?"

"First, there's the hearing. Vinny wants to be sure you'll do everything you can to make sure Nick don't get sent to Italy or nothin' like that."

She'd expected something like this, but she didn't think Vinny would feel the need to issue a threat, if that's what this was. "You can assure Mr. Antonelli I'll do the very best I can."

"Good, Mrs. Mondavi, real good." He rubbed his grizzled chin.

"Is there anything else?"

"Yes, Mrs. Mondavi, there's . . . well, there ain't no way to say it but say it. Vinny wants to know if you told Nicky about the little problem with your father."

"If you mean did I tell Nick I was blackmailed into marrying him, the answer is no."

"Hey, that's great, Mrs. Mondavi. Terrific!"

"I'm glad you're so pleased."

"You've lived up to your end of the bargain, and Vinny is truly grateful." Louie reached inside his coat and removed an envelope. "In accordance with the agreement, Vinny wants you to have this."

She took the envelope from him. There was no writing on it.

"Go ahead and look inside if you want."

Felicia opened it. The envelope contained a check made out to her for a quarter of a million dollars. It was drawn on the account of a bank in the Cayman Islands.

"For services rendered," Louie said, bouncing on his toes and looking a bit smug. "Vinny asked me to give his heartfelt thanks, Mrs. Mondavi, and to offer his congratulations."

Felicia was still a bit numb as she stared at the check. She'd never seen one that big in her life. A part of her had doubted she'd ever see the money. "Thank you," she stammered. "Tell Mr. Antonelli thank you for me."

"Sure will." He grinned again, glancing at her legs.

Felicia waited, expecting him to say he would leave, but he remained rooted to the spot. She started feeling uncomfortable when he just stood there with a painful grin on his face.

"Is there something else?" she asked stiffly.

"Yeah, Mrs. Mondavi, a request, I guess you could say."

"Yes?"

"Since Nicky is so happy and he seems to love you and all that, well, Vinny thinks it would be a shame if Nicky heard about the little problem with your father."

"I told you I haven't said a word. To anyone."

"Yes, Mrs. Mondavi, but as you and Nicky get closer and it gets easier to talk and, well, you might slip. And if you do, then Nicky could get ticked. The point is that Vinny wants good relations with Nicky. Do you get my drift?"

"You're saying if I tell Nick his uncle blackmailed me, something very unpleasant might happen."

"Uh, I wouldn't be quite that—"

"Don't whitewash it, Louie. Just say it. If I talk you'll slash my face? Kill my father? Throw my mother off a cliff?"

Louie grimaced, not looking pleased at all. "I think we understand each other, Mrs. Mondavi. Right now that's all that matters." Again he looked her over. "So I'll be going and let you get back to your cookies."

She waited as Louie went to the door.

"Oh, and Vinny wanted me to remind you that if there's a little Mondavi around soon to eat those cookies, there'll be another check. A hundred thousand if you get in a family way."

Felicia blushed.

Louie grinned. "You see, we ain't so bad. You scratch Vinny's back, he scratches yours." He glanced at the chandelier again. "Meanwhile you get to live in this nice house and enjoy, knowin' there's lots of scratch in the bank. There's a million broads that'd change places with you in a minute, Mrs. Mondavi." Louie gave her a casual salute and went out the door.

Felicia closed her eyes. For a minute she couldn't move. Her heart was pounding so hard it hurt. Then she looked at the check. She had a sudden, overwhelming urge to rip the damned thing to shreds. The last thing she wanted was a reminder of the reality behind her marriage to Nick. On the other hand, it was little enough compensation for what her family had been through. But to take the money was like admitting it had been important to her. Worse, just holding it in her hand made her feel cheap and ashamed.

She was about to go upstairs and put the check away when she heard a key in the door. She quickly stuffed the check in her pocket as the door swung open. It was Nick with a bouquet of flowers in his hand.

"Nick! You're home early."

He had a quizzical expression on his face. "Who was the guy who just left?"

"Nobody," she said, caught completely off guard.

"Nobody?" he said, putting the flowers down on the hall table.

"What I meant was, nobody important. His name's Louie. I don't even know his last name."

"Well, what did Louie want? Don't tell me he was selling magazines."

"Nick, you aren't jealous, are you?"

"Should I be?"

"No, of course not."

"So?" he said, waiting.

She agonized, wondering how to explain.

"Felicia?"

She sighed, realizing there was no point in lying. "Louie works for your uncle," she said, going into the front room. Nick followed her.

"So, what did he want?"

Felicia gave him a look as she sat on the sofa. "To see how things were going between us."

Nick gave her a skeptical look. "Uncle Vinny sent a goon to ask how things are going? Come on, give me a break."

"It's true."

"Well, what did you tell him?"

She agonized again. "That things were fine."

"And that's it? Louie came to ask how things are going, you told him fine and he went away happy?"

"Yes."

He stood before her, studying her for a long time. "I really hate to say this, Felicia, but I don't believe you're telling me the truth. At least not the whole truth."

"Oh, Nick," she said with a sigh, "can't you let it go? Why are you putting me on the spot?"

"I suppose because I'd like to trust my own wife," he said, his tone more pointed than before. "You're hiding something."

"Nick..."

"Well, aren't you?"

Felicia got to her feet. "I've got to get my brownies in the oven or we won't have dessert tonight."

Nick grabbed her wrist as she went by, stopping her. She looked into his eyes. His expression hardened.

"Don't walk out on me," he said, sounding as though he was forcing an unnatural calmness to his voice.

"Nick, please." Wrenching herself free, she went to the kitchen.

He was right on her heels. "You're not leveling with me," he said, "and I don't appreciate it."

She stopped and turned on her heel. Her hands went defiantly to her hips. "You're too damned stubborn for your own good. Don't you know that sometimes everyone's better off if you just let things drop?"

"I can see how you might feel that way. But I'm the one who doesn't know what the hell's going on."

Nick was glaring, his face red. She knew they were headed for disaster. But what could she do? She went to the stove to melt her chocolate.

He came up beside her, getting in her face. "Felicia, you're lying to me about a man I found you alone with in my house, and I want to know what was going on."

"Good Lord," she screamed, throwing down a hot pad, "what do you think? That I was having an affair with him? That I'd sleep with somebody I didn't even know?"

"Well, it didn't stop you from sleeping with me, did it?"

She was so furious she'd slapped him before her brain could stop her. She'd hit him hard enough to knock him back half a step.

"Well," he said, drawing himself up. "Nice to see you have limits. For a minute there, I was worried."

"Nick, you're a bastard," she said, seething. "A real bastard."

"And what are *you*, Felicia? That's the topic of discussion, I believe."

"Oh, how can you treat me this way?" she cried, tears filling her eyes. "You couldn't. Not if you care for me."

"It has nothing to do with caring for you. It has to do with you refusing to tell the truth."

"All right," she sobbed, digging into her pocket. Jerking out the check, she stuffed it into his hand. "See for yourself."

He looked at the check, his brows rising. "Two hundred and fifty thousand?"

"I hope you're satisfied," she said bitterly.

"This is from Vinny?"

"Yes."

"This is what he gave you to marry me?"

"Yes."

Nick's expression turned hard. "No wonder you didn't want to tell me. It's payday."

She glared.

"Congratulations. Anybody who can wring that kind of money out of Vincent Antonelli deserves a pat on the back. Or the ass."

She clenched her fists, but this time she restrained herself. Tears, angry tears gushed from her eyes. "I didn't want to rub your nose in it," she sobbed. "But I don't know why I bothered. You've considered me a gold digger from the day we met. You've been patronizing me since then. As least now you're being honest."

Nick looked at the check. "And so, my dear, are you." He shook his head with disgust. "I've got to hand it to you, your performance the past few days was so inspired I actually forgot why you married me. Here's your paycheck, sweetheart," he said, stuffing the check down the front of her T-shirt. "You've earned it."

She couldn't believe the hateful things he was saying. She was so hurt, so angry, her entire body shook.

"Save the tears for your banker. I know too much."

She was crying so hard she couldn't speak.

"Maybe I am too honest about my feelings," he said coldly. "And maybe I'm a fool, as well. But one good thing about this. At least we understand each other now. I won't take anything you say or do too seriously in the future." Turning on his heel, he walked from the room.

Felicia pulled Vinny's check from her shirt. A tear dropped onto his signature, smearing the ink. Cursing him, she crumpled the check. Had there been a fire, she'd have thrown the check into it without hesitating.

Instead, she opened it, folded it neatly and put it in her pocket. Because of Vincent Antonelli she would come out

of this marriage with nothing but money. Though she'd
been unwilling and innocent, the fact was the man had
turned her into a whore. Nick felt that way about her
now—that was clear enough—and he'd never see her any
other way again.

THEY ATE DINNER in stony silence. Felicia felt handcuffed,
helpless. Nick was not unkind. He did not ridicule her or
give her contemptuous looks. Vinny's check was not
mentioned. What little conversation they had was about
the house and Nick's schedule for the next few days.

The flowers Nick had brought remained on the table in
the entry hall. In the morning, after he had gone to work,
she would throw them in the garbage. Until then, they
would stay where they were, a symbol of their failed marriage. For that's what it was. Had it not been for Nick's
immigration hearing, there wouldn't be a reason for her
to stay in the house. The last few idyllic days were gone
forever.

Why should she be surprised? Their happiness had been
based on lies and deception, pretense and folly. They were
victims, yes, but that didn't change a thing.

Nick stayed up reading until long after Felicia had
turned off the lights and gone to bed. She was awake when
he climbed in bed, though she didn't let him know. It was
a long time after he was snoring that she finally fell asleep.

When she went down to breakfast in the morning, Nick
was already gone. She found the flowers he'd brought in
a vase on the kitchen table. They were a bit wilted. There
was a note under the vase and a key next to it. The note
read,

Felicia,
I'm sorry I hurt you last night. My disappointment
was no reason to have been so unkind. I see in retrospect that you did nothing I hadn't already known

about. You told me the first day we met that you'd
been offered a great deal of money to marry me. The
problem was, I tried to convince myself that it wasn't
so. You can't be blamed for my self-delusion. And so
I apologize.

I would like to put your mind at ease about one thing.
I won't hold you to this marriage once my problems
with the government are behind me. Whichever way
things work out, you will be free to go. In the meantime whatever you can do to help with the INS would
be appreciated. But rest assured, with me you don't
have to pretend.

This key is to the gate at Gramercy Park. I got it as a
present but see no reason you shouldn't have it, despite our change of circumstances. Perhaps the park
will give you pleasure.

Nick

Felicia could hardly hate him after his gesture of kindness. He was generous and conciliatory, which she greatly
appreciated. And he was right to want to end the pretense. To sleep with him and act as if nothing had happened would have been impossible for her, because it
would have been so terribly false. Nick didn't know it, but
the unspoken truth behind her reasons for marrying him
would always stand between them. Never again could she
pretend that what Vinny had done to her and her father
didn't matter.

Any love that had begun to blossom between her and
Nick had withered and was gone. It was dead. It was over.
There was no way it could survive.

During the ensuing week Nick was true to his promise.
He was polite, businesslike, but distant. They talked only
about practical matters. They never laughed. It seemed
even their friendship was over.

Felicia spent empty days going to the park, cooking meals that Nick frequently didn't come home to eat. Matti knew there was something wrong, but Felicia had no intention of discussing it with her. Their relationship dissolved to cool formality. Somehow she found that easier.

Maria Antonelli telephoned a couple of times, suggesting lunch or shopping. Felicia politely put her off. It would have been too painful to pretend around her, though the day might come when she had little choice.

Nearly every day she called her mother, who could tell by her tone that all was not well. Felicia didn't explain. She simply passed the problem off as the difficulties of newlyweds. Nick was very busy, she said, and preoccupied.

One afternoon she was able to talk to her father when her mother wasn't around. Carlo was concerned that Nick had been unkind to her.

"No, Pops," she said, "his ego won't let him forget I was bought, that's all. It's just a marriage of convenience."

"Convenient for him, maybe," Carlo groused.

"It's all right," she told her father. "Really, I'm fine."

"I've heard that tone in your voice before, Felicia. After Johnny Fano. It wasn't true then, it isn't true now."

"Think what you want. I'm okay. Nobody puts demands on me. I'm no worse off than I was before."

Of course, there was one thing different. For one idyllic week she'd been in love ... or thought she was. Maybe she'd kidded herself, but to her it seemed that so long as she and Nick kept the reasons for their marriage from their minds, they'd been as happy as any other newlyweds. That was one thing Nick had been wrong about. She hadn't been acting. She loved him and thought he loved her, too. Proof how blind love could be. It had happened with Johnny Fano. Now, with Nick, it had happened again.

NICK STOOD at his office window, staring down through the Venetian blinds at the street. A few days ago he'd stood in the same spot, regretting every minute he spent at work, wishing he was home with Felicia. Now it pained him to think of going back there. He'd used every excuse he could to avoid it. Being with her was like being with the living dead.

Though he'd been angry with her for the disappointment he'd suffered, he'd soon realized that she'd not done anything wrong. Felicia hadn't lied—she'd let him have him his illusions. In other words, she'd done her job too well.

Nick couldn't hate her for being who she was. An awful lot of women would have taken the quarter of a million to do what she was asked to do. No, he realized, if there was a problem, it was that he'd deceived himself.

Not that his feelings for her hadn't been genuine. The problem was they were built on shifting sand. Everything from beginning to end was one big fraud, and he'd contributed to it as much as Felicia.

The past several days he'd been telling himself to treat her as a business proposition, which was what Vinny had intended from the start. The INS was hounding him. He needed her, and she was prepared to do her job. But it wasn't easy to be around her. He had to force himself to focus on who and what she really was—not the beautiful woman, the illusion he'd come to love.

The intercom on the desk behind him buzzed and Nick turned, surprised by the sound. Funny how even at his office, the world of reality seemed intrusive. Felicia—the illusory Felicia—had so consumed his thoughts that everything else seemed a distraction.

Nick picked up the phone. "Yes?"

"Mr. Mondavi," the receptionist said, "there's a gentleman with the government here to see you. A Mr. Wilkins."

"What's it regarding?"

"He said he has some papers for you. He'd like to give them to you personally."

"All right," Nick said. "Send him in."

He went around the desk as the door opened. A ruddy-faced man in a brown suit came in the door.

"Mr. Nicolo P. Mondavi?" he said.

"Yes, I'm Nick Mondavi."

"Lance Wilkins," the man said, introducing himself. "I have some papers here ordering you to appear before an administrative hearing of the Immigration and Naturalization Service on the twenty-second of the month." He handed Nick a manila envelope. "The hearing officer has been in contact with your attorney, but regulations require that you be personally served." The man smiled wanly. "I was in the neighborhood."

Nick looked at the envelope. "So this is the shot across my bow."

"I'd say that occurred a while back, Mr. Mondavi. This is more like the first broadside." He grinned. "Off the record, of course."

"In other words, see you in court."

Wilkins nodded. "That's it." He turned and went to the door. "Have a good day, Mr. Mondavi."

Nick tossed the envelope onto his desk and returned to the window. In the street below he saw a shapely brunette, her short skirt fluttering in the wind. She didn't look like Felicia, but she was reminiscent of her. He felt the same old clench in his gut that usually accompanied thoughts of his wife. Damn Vincent Antonelli to hell.

Nick went to his desk, took the phone and dialed. When Helen Stevens came on the line he said, "I just got served by the INS, Helen."

"Yes, I'm aware," she said.

"It's official, then."

"Yes, Nick," the lawyer told him. "We're at war."

AS THE STRAINED feelings between her and Nick went into a second week—and his hearing date grew closer—Felicia grew more and more tense. On top of everything else, she had missed her period, which normally was no big deal. She was often late, especially if she'd been under stress. But the possibility that she might be pregnant became yet another worry. After all, they hadn't used birth control.

Lord knew, a baby was the last thing she needed at this point. Oddly enough, when they first became estranged, Felicia had assumed the chance of a pregnancy happening was behind her. What she hadn't counted on was that it had already happened—sometime between their wedding night and the day Louie came to the house.

With each passing day, she grew more and more concerned. She and Nick didn't talk a lot, and she didn't want to share her worries with him until she was sure. He was preoccupied with his work, and there had been complications regarding his hearing. The hearing officer moved the date back a few days, which meant their agony could not end.

Though it was still early for a home pregnancy test to be fully accurate, she purchased one. When it came up positive, she broke into a cold sweat. Vinny would be pleased, and maybe Helen Stevens, Nick's attorney, but probably not Nick. He didn't need this complication any more than she did.

The next day, Felicia took a taxi to Planned Parenthood. The lab confirmed her worst fears. Sitting home that afternoon, anguishing, it didn't take long to make up her mind. She'd tell Nick and get it over with. There were already too many secrets between them. Besides, he was entitled to know.

She paced the front room, waiting for him to arrive. He hadn't said anything about not being home for dinner, so when it grew late, she wondered where he could be. "Damn it, Nick," she muttered, "not tonight."

After another half hour the phone rang. If it was Nick saying he wouldn't be home for dinner, she'd just tell him over the phone. She couldn't go on any longer.

"Hello?" she said, snatching the receiver in his study.

"Felicia?" It was her mother's voice and it was trembling.

"Mama?"

"Honey, it's your papa . . . he's had a heart attack."

"Oh, my God!"

"He's in the hospital and he's okay, they think. But it was a very serious one this time. The doctors say the next day or so will be critical."

"Oh, Mama," she cried as the tears filled her eyes and began running down her cheeks. "No, no . . ."

Just then, Felicia heard the front door open. She turned to the entrance of the study as her mother spoke. Nick appeared in the doorway. Seeing she was crying, he stepped into the room, alarm on his face.

"What happened? What's wrong?"

Felicia put her hand on the mouthpiece. "My father," she said, her voice trembling. "He's had another heart attack."

"Who's that? Your mom?"

She nodded and began weeping. She tried to say something to her mother, but couldn't. She handed Nick the phone.

"Louisa, this is Nick. How serious is it?" He listened for several moments, then said, "Don't worry. I'll have her on the next flight out. I'll call back with the details. Give me the number at the hospital."

He wrote it down, thanked her and hung up. Felicia stood there, her face buried in her hands. Nick stepped forward and put his arms around her.

"I can't go," she said, sobbing. "Your hearing is in two days."

"The hell with the hearing. Go to your father, Felicia. Go to your father."

Felicia refused and had her fingers free, but instead it made Nick enjoy the most caring, most of his recovery. She was terribly relieved and cried like him and felt sorry. There had been the worst few weeks of her life. And Felicia knew where she and each of her money could buy her another tomorrow.

Felicia and Nick travel up to the Los Angeles Mercy Hospital in Daly City, just the seventh being that was not dead by then. In the hospital and the day with her finding the spot where Felicia took her ticket on the liver lesions, until Felicia at gasped, but she again not seen off her hand.

On the plane she decided not to think she should either do something about being free, but, but there was no doubt. Only to take decided everything. Nick put on his hat that not endeavored. A few days to distract the passengers, Felicia had enough to think about. She would know that the seats to the time he got in.

The love that had given her pleasure of her further spoke her mind and then found Nick's legal problems would be every certainly though not at exactly the day of the hearing. Nick thought, they could afford out. He smashes, if that was the that mean this a try to continue. While the pressure of justice slowly beautifully near. Could she raise within an the problem would like neither she or sit figure? I felt face with the doubts. Give me the number at the copyright, there was not the least of which

# 13

BY THE TIME Felicia reached San Francisco, her father had already survived the most critical phase of his recovery. She was terribly relieved and cried in her mother's arms. These had been the worst few weeks of her life, yet Felicia couldn't share the full extent of her misery with her own mother. Even now.

Carlo had been transferred to the heart unit at Mary Seton Hospital in Daly City, near the airport. Felicia had taken a taxi directly to the hospital, not knowing what she'd find until she got there. Louisa took her to the cardiac intensive care unit. Carlo was asleep, but she kissed him and held his hand.

On the plane, she'd agonized over whether she should tell her mother about being pregnant, but since Nick didn't know yet, she decided she couldn't risk having him find out accidentally. A few days wouldn't matter. Besides, the family had enough to think about. She would keep it her secret for the time being.

The long flight had also given her plenty of time to think about her child and the future. Nick's legal problems would be over eventually, though not necessarily the day of the hearing. With appeals they could grind out for months, if not years. Did that mean they'd be in purgatory while the wheels of justice slowly ground along? Could she raise a child in that atmosphere? How would Nick feel about it?

There were so many unknowns, not the least of which

was her father's health. Felicia felt as though the world was closing in on her.

She insisted on staying at the hospital, even though her father had been asleep the whole time. Her mother hadn't had dinner, so she went to the cafeteria.

Seated at Carlo's bedside, Felicia had a long conversation with him in her mind, telling him everything that had happened and seeking his support and comfort. The problem was her poor father regarded himself as the cause of her suffering and, had the conversation been real, he would try to take her burdens on himself, which was the last thing he needed. And so she could only pretend.

Her mother came back from dinner and put her hand on Felicia's shoulder. "The nurse says your papa could sleep for hours. Come home and rest. We can come back in the morning."

"But Mama, you spent the first night with him, I should spend tonight."

"It's not necessary. You need your rest. Your mama knows best, Felicia."

It was almost as though at some level her mother knew she was pregnant, though of course she couldn't. Mothers sometimes sensed things they didn't fully understand. She, too, would be in that situation soon. A mother. Unfortunately, the prospect brought as much pain as joy. How terribly sad that was. She looked into her mother's eyes.

"All right, Mama, whatever you say." Felicia pushed the oxygen tube aside and kissed her father's cheek. "Sleep well, Pops. I'll see you in the morning," she whispered.

NICK CAME OUT of the terminal building and headed straight for the taxi stand. He had no idea where Daly City was, but he was relieved to discover it wasn't far, closer even than San Francisco proper.

Nick went to the cardiac unit, and the nurse at the desk told him he'd missed his wife and mother-in-law by half an hour. It wasn't until that moment that he realized how badly he'd wanted to see Felicia and how disappointed he was at having missed her.

True, he'd come to San Francisco out of a sense of duty, but this crisis made him mentally push their problems aside. Despite everything, he just could not get that other Felicia, the one he had fallen in love with, out of his mind.

"How's Carlo?" he asked the nurse.

"Doing well. Would you like to see him, Mr. Mondavi? He woke a short time ago and asked about his family."

Nick could hardly say no, though he was sure Carlo would have no desire to see him. But he figured if he could put his mind at ease about Felicia, it would be worth it. The nurse pointed him to the intensive care unit, and Nick went in. Carlo seemed surprised to see him.

"I just arrived," Nick explained, approaching the bed. "Thought if I could be of help I ought to come."

"They told me Felicia arrived this afternoon, but I was sleeping. I didn't get to see her."

"Rotten luck to see me instead."

Carlo studied him. "Maybe it's just as well, Nick."

"Why's that?"

"Yesterday, laying in this bed, not knowing whether I was going to live or die, I thought of my life . . . the good things and the bad. There was one thing that tore at my soul, a problem I have not solved. I don't want to die without taking care of it. That's why I'm glad to see you. Maybe God sent you."

"I'm not sure I understand."

"Of course you don't." He pointed at the chair next to the bed. "Sit down, Nick."

He sat in the chair.

"I want to ask you a simple question," Carlo said. "I want an honest answer. Nothing less will do."

Nick waited.

"Do you love my daughter?"

Nick was caught off guard. For a moment he didn't speak. Carlo's eyes were fearless as he studied him, waiting.

"There are many reasons for me not to love her, Carlo, but the truth is, I do. I'll be honest. I hate the fact that it's true, but I do love Felicia."

Carlo sighed. "Good."

"I'm glad you feel that way, but there's not a lot of reason to be pleased, believe me."

"Nick, I should have told you this the day you came to the restaurant, but I didn't because I was afraid. Not for myself. For Felicia."

Nick saw a certainty in the man's eyes he hadn't seen before. It was the look of a person who'd stared death in the face. He'd seen it in Gina's eyes before she'd lapsed into a coma. People were changed by these momentous occasions.

"Told me what, Carlo?"

"The truth about Vinny and Felicia. But first, I want you to promise me you won't let anything happen to her. I want your word that as her husband you'll protect her."

There was an unmistakably ominous quality in Carlo's tone. "What about Felicia?"

"She didn't marry you for money. She married you to save my life. Your uncle would have killed me and maybe done unspeakable things to Felicia if she didn't agree to marry you."

"What?"

"It's true. Vinny was claiming a favor. I owed your uncle a life, Nick. But instead of mine, he asked for my daughter's."

"What are you saying?"

"Forty years ago I made a terrible mistake," Carlo said. "And now my daughter, the joy of my life, was made to

pay for my sin. If you love her as you say, then you, as her
husband, must know the truth. Should Vinny want my life
for what I'm telling you, then he can have it. But you can
save Felicia, Nick. I am trusting you to save her life."

FELICIA WASN'T UP to a lot of conversation with her
mother—not considering how much she had to keep from
her—so she went straight to bed. Louisa was tired, too, but
she said she wanted to stay up to make some minestrone.
"I don't know if the doctors will let Carlo have any, but I'm
going to make it just in case."

Louisa used cooking as a form of therapy. Felicia recalled from her years growing up that in time of sadness
or stress her mother would cook compulsively to help
herself cope.

Lying in the bed that had been hers until she'd gotten her
own apartment, Felicia marveled at the chain of events
that had brought her full circle, back to her parents' home.
She was a completely changed woman, however. She'd
been touched by love, but also by deep sorrow. She was
pregnant by a man who couldn't love her. Fate had forced
them to be unloving and unkind. Neither of them de-
served what they'd done to each other, but it had happened, and there was nothing to be done now but endure.

She had begun drifting off to sleep, the first delightful
smells of her mother's cooking reaching her nose, when
she heard the doorbell sound. It was late for a visitor, but
the answering machine was full of messages from concerned friends when they got home. It was probably a
neighbor.

Felicia was glad. Her mother would have someone to
talk to as she cooked. She hadn't been a good daughter in
that regard, though if her mother knew the burdens she
was carrying, she'd certainly have understood.

As she lay there, Felicia thought she heard the sound of
a man's voice. Could it be their parish priest? Father Se-

bastian, her mother said, had been out of town when Carlo had his attack. Maybe he'd come back and was calling to offer his comfort.

But then the bedroom door opened, spilling light from the hallway into the room.

"Felicia?" her mother said softly. "Are you awake?"

"Yes, Mama, what's wrong?"

"Your husband's here. He wants to talk to you."

"Nick's here?"

"Yes, honey. He's very anxious. Do you want to come out, or should I have him come back?"

Felicia couldn't imagine why Nick would be there and what he would be upset about, but she was sure she didn't want her mother to hear whatever it was he had to say. Louisa had enough on her mind as it was.

"Ask him to come in, Mama, but give me one minute."

Felicia got up and slipped on her bathrobe. Then she checked herself in the dresser mirror—the same mirror in which she'd fussed over herself countless hours as a teenager. She ran a brush through her hair and put it down when there was a soft knock.

"Come in," she said.

The door opened. Nick looked tired and concerned, but not angry, as she half expected. Actually, she hadn't known what to expect. The fact that he was there was a tremendous shock.

"Nick, what are you doing here?"

He stepped inside, closed the door, then faced her. She could see by his expression that something was wrong.

"Nick?"

"I've just come from the hospital, Felicia. I spoke with your father."

"But why? What are you doing here?"

"I flew out here because I felt badly and wanted to see if I could help. I came for you, but when you weren't at the hospital I looked in on your dad. We had a very frank conversation. He told me about him and Vinny and the favor. He told me you were blackmailed into marrying me. He told me everything."

"Oh, my God."

"Don't worry. Nothing's going to happen because of it. I won't let it."

She clasped her hands at her breast, dropping onto the bed. She began trembling.

"Felicia," Nick said, pulling a chair over and sitting in front of her, "I can't tell you how ashamed I am. I've never felt so vile, so despicable in my life."

"It wasn't your fault, Nick."

"But the way I treated you, the things I said . . . Why didn't you tell me? Why did you let me go on torturing and ridiculing you when you were an innocent victim?"

"I had no choice, Nick."

"But didn't you know I'd have done whatever was necessary to spare you?"

"I wasn't sure there was anything you could do. Besides, they made it very clear if I told you I was blackmailed there'd be dire consequences. Louie said if you ever found out . . . Well, I don't think I have to explain."

Nick reached out and took her hand. "I feel awful about this. If I'd known, I'd never have married you. I honestly thought you were doing it for the money."

She knew that remark could be taken several ways, but then she was aware long before now that Nick wasn't the primary cause of her problems. "We're both victims in a way," she assured him. "I've felt that all along."

"How could you not have hated me, the way I treated you?"

"You'd made reasonable assumptions. I was aware of that."

"Still . . ."

"Don't beat yourself over it, Nick. Now we both know the truth. Personally, I feel a huge burden has been removed."

He shook his head sadly. "There's only one thing for me to do now—undo this as best I can. I realize some things can't be undone, but anything that's in my power will be taken care of. There's no reason why our marriage can't be annulled, for example. What better justification is there than a woman being blackmailed? Just tell me what you want, and I'll see that it's done."

"What about your immigration case?"

"How could I expect you to help me, when all this time you must have been loathing me? I can only imagine."

Felicia bit her lip. "It must not have been a picnic for you, either."

"There was one big difference. Nobody was twisting my arm."

"Your uncle put pressure on you, too," she insisted.

"Not like what you faced," he said with an embarrassed laugh. "And it's not like I wasn't willing to take advantage of the situation. There was no reason we had to make love, but I was both cynical and selfish. You were beautiful, and I used you. There's no excuse for that."

Her eyes bubbled with tears.

"Being a party to your exploitation is one of the lowest moments of my life. I can't blame you for hating me."

"I don't hate you, Nick."

"I wish you did. It would almost make it easier. As it is, I don't know how you endured what my family did to you."

Tears overflowed her lids. Nick rubbed the backs of her hands with his thumbs.

"Maybe I do know. You loved your father and refused to let anything happen to him." Nick bowed his head. "I know I have no right to expect it, but I hope someday you'll find it in your heart to forgive me."

"Don't talk like this. It makes it worse."

"You're right," he said, getting to his feet. "I'm worrying more about my own guilty conscience than your well-being. I'll leave. But first, I want to assure you that you and your family will have absolutely nothing to fear from my uncle."

"Nick, promise me you won't get upset with him. That's the one thing he cares about. Tell him you decided you didn't like me. Tell him anything but the truth."

"I'll do whatever makes you feel better."

"You can't let him know we told you about the blackmail."

"All right. But I have learned one thing from this ordeal—that I can't rely on anyone else to solve my problems for me. I'll be nice to my uncle for your sake, Felicia, but this will be the last time I ever deal with him. I know that's little comfort to you, but at this point there's not much I can do that's constructive. The damage has been done."

Felicia bowed her head. His remorse was nearly as painful as his rejection. What he'd said earlier kept running through her mind. *If I'd known, I'd never have married you.* That, indeed, was the bottom line. "At least we can part feeling better about each other," she said.

"You're far too generous, Felicia."

"Thank you for coming to me like this. I know you didn't have to."

He reached out and touched her cheek, drawing his fingers slowly over her skin. What was it she saw in his eyes? Why were they shimmering? She wanted it to be love, but she couldn't say it was. Nick was a good and decent man. Of that much she could be sure. That must have been what motivated him—a desire to do the right thing. His nobility was admirable, but what she wanted was his love. Why couldn't he see that?

"When I get back to New York," he said, "I'll talk to the church and sort out the technicalities of the annulment. That'll be important to your mother, I'm sure."

A tear dropped onto her lap, and she nodded.

"Forgive me, Felicia," he said, his voice cracking. "I'm terribly, terribly sorry."

Then he left. She sat there on her bed for a long time, tears streaking down her cheeks. How ironic. Even in victory she suffered.

IN THE MORNING Felicia told her mother the entire story—except for the fact she was pregnant. Louisa did not chastise her for keeping the truth from her, though she did say that had she known, she might have better helped Carlo bear his pain.

Felicia sighed. "The point now is it's over and behind us."

"I will grieve for you, Felicia," her mother told her. "For the rest of my days."

After breakfast they went to the hospital to see Carlo. He was much better, according to the nurses, but there was worry on his face. "How did it go with Nick?" he asked, casting a worried glance in the direction of his wife.

"Don't worry, Carlo," Louisa told him. "I know everything."

Felicia told him about Nick's visit to the house and of his offer to do what he could to right the wrongs. Louisa shook her head, lamenting as Felicia recounted the events of the previous evening. Carlo didn't seem as pleased as Felicia expected.

"Aren't you glad, Pops?"

"Well, I'm a little confused," he said. "It sounds like a strange way for a man to behave. If he loves you, why should he want to annul the marriage?"

"What makes you think he loves me?"

"He told me so," Carlo replied.

"What?"

"I wouldn't have said anything to him unless I was satisfied he loved you, so I asked him first."

"And Nick said he loved me?"

"Yes."

"It must have been because he didn't want to upset you."

"No, I'm sure he meant it. Anyway, he was aware I didn't believe you'd married for love. Don't forget I'd told him once before you did it for the money. But this time I told him the truth."

She wondered why Nick hadn't said anything about that. Was it because he didn't want to cause more pain? Or did he assume that since she was blackmailed, she'd never had feelings for him?

What a terrible mess.

Felicia spent the afternoon with her father. Both his conversation with Nick and their conversation that morning had done wonders for him. His color was better than it had been in months. Carlo was clearly relieved.

Louisa also seemed in better spirits. "I knew something was wrong between you and Nick," she said, as they walked the halls during Carlo's nap, "I just didn't know what. But what a shame he wants to annul the marriage even though he loves you."

"Maybe it's not true. Nick is a kind person underneath. We were happy long enough for me to know that. He might have said that for Pop's benefit. Honestly, what's he going to do? Tell a sick man he hates his daughter?"

"Nick doesn't hate you, Felicia. This I know. I saw his face when he left last night. He was in pain."

Felicia agonized all evening. Even after she and her mother were assured that Carlo was out of danger and would likely have a full recovery, she was upset. It was one less worry, but it also made her wonder if her place wasn't really in that courtroom with Nick.

After dinner she phoned the airlines to see if she could get on the red-eye flight to Kennedy International. Two hours later, her mother was dropping her off at the airport.

"Tell Pops I'd have stayed another day, but Nick's hearing is tomorrow morning."

"He'll understand. What your father wants more than anything is for you to be happy. That's why he's been so miserable these last weeks."

Felicia embraced her mother. "I'll call as soon as I have news," she said, getting out of the car.

"Be honest with him," Louisa called after her. "That's always best."

NICK ONLY HALF listened as Helen Stevens addressed the hearing officer. It had been a major struggle for him even to get to the federal building that morning. He'd felt empty and bereft since leaving San Francisco. Nothing seemed to matter to him since he'd set Felicia free.

His attention was brought back when the hearing officer addressed the matter of his marital status. Helen was in the middle of explaining that Felicia had been called to her sick father's bedside in San Francisco when the door of the hearing room opened and Felicia walked in.

Nick was stunned. Helen asked for a brief recess. Felicia approached the table where he and Helen sat. He got to his feet.

"Hi," she said, giving him a brief smile.

"How's your father?"

"Much better. Well enough that I thought I should be here. Am I too late, Helen?" she asked the lawyer.

"Your timing couldn't be better, actually," Helen replied. "This is when I would have put you on."

"I'm ready to testify," she said.

"Felicia," Nick said, "I don't want you to feel you have to do this. You have no obligation to me or anyone else."

"I'm here because I want to be, Nick." She opened her purse, took out a check folded in half and handed it to him. "Give this to your uncle," she said. "I don't want it. The thought of where it came from would spoil any pleasure it might bring me."

Nick looked at Uncle Vinny's check. The pain in his heart cut still deeper. Why had she come?

But he didn't have time to think about it, because Helen was telling the hearing officer that Mrs. Mondavi had arrived and was prepared to testify. The officer instructed the clerk to swear Felicia in. Helen questioned her first.

"Tell us about your marriage, Mrs. Mondavi," she said. "Start with your reasons for marrying, and the circumstances."

"I probably wouldn't have married him if it wasn't for our families," Felicia began. "By many standards I was a spinster. My parents had been hoping for years I'd find someone. Nick's aunt heard I was available, so to speak, and saw a picture of me. She showed it to Nick, and from what I'm told he fell for what he saw in the photo. He flew to San Francisco at his aunt's urging. We met, and in a matter of days he asked me to marry him."

"Were you in love with him?" Helen asked. "Is that why you accepted his offer of marriage?"

"No. I was attracted to Nick from the start. He seemed a decent guy. And the fact that he was well off didn't hurt. But family pressures played a bigger role than anything."

"Did Mr. Mondavi offer you any inducement to marry?"

"No."

"Did he inform you of the possibility of an action against him under the immigration laws?"

"Yes."

"Did he propose the possibility of a sham marriage?"

"No, just the opposite. He said a sham marriage would be pointless. He said his desire was that we live as man and wife."

"Did you?"

"We have a sexual relationship, as married people usually do," Felicia replied, glancing at Nick.

He lowered his eyes.

"Would you say you love your husband, Mrs. Mondavi?"

"Yes, I do."

Nick looked up, surprise on his face.

"So, would you characterize your relationship as normal?" Helen asked.

"I don't know if there is any such thing as normal. Each relationship is different, it seems to me. But there are certain things people who are married tend to do, and I'd say Nick and I did them."

"Could you be more specific, Mrs. Mondavi?" the hearing officer said.

"Yes, sir. I guess the best example of what I'm saying is that I'm pregnant. Nick and I are going to have a baby."

Nick's mouth dropped open. She couldn't help but smile.

"You may have noticed that Nick is surprised," she said to the hearing officer. "That's because I didn't have a chance to tell him before I left to be with my father. I'd just gotten the test results." She opened her purse. "I have the paper they gave me here, if you need the evidence."

"That's quite all right, Mrs. Mondavi," the officer said. "That isn't necessary." He chuckled. "I must say, this is the first time I've been a party to this kind of news being given to an expectant father. How about you, counsel?"

Helen Stevens smiled. The INS attorney shrugged.

"Ms. Stevens," the hearing officer said, "any more questions for Mrs. Mondavi?"

"None."

"Mr. Weintraub, would the government care to examine the witness?"

"A point of clarification," he said. "Mrs. Mondavi, you said you received no inducement for marrying your husband."

"I said he didn't offer any."

"Did a third party do so?"

"Let me say this, if anyone offered me money to marry Nick, I'd return it. I had my own selfish motives for accepting his proposal, but I came to love him. There's nobody in the world I'd rather be married to."

The lawyer took his seat. "No further questions."

"You're excused, Mrs. Mondavi," the officer said. He looked over his half-frame glasses at the clock. "Perhaps we can recess for lunch, ladies and gentlemen. If it's agreeable, we'll reconvene at two."

The hearing officer left the room as the others, including Helen Stevens, gathered their things. Nick and Felicia continued to stare at each other. She remained in the witness chair, Nick at the table. Helen put her hand on his shoulder.

"I'll leave you to process the happy news," she said. "Incidentally, congratulations."

Helen left with the others. Felicia still hadn't moved.

"The judge didn't give me the opportunity to ask," Nick said, "but I have one question for the witness."

"What's that?"

"Is it true?"

"Yes, I've got the pregnancy test result right here. Want to see it?" she said, holding out the paper.

"No, that's not what I meant. I meant, was it true when you said you loved me?"

Felicia nodded. "That was the truest thing I said."

Nick got to his feet, and she did, as well. He rushed to her and they embraced. He squeezed her hard and kissed her face. She pulled back.

"But I've got a question for you. Did you mean it when you told my father you loved me?"

Nick shook his head helplessly, his eyes shining. "It's the truest thing I ever said."

They embraced again. The feel of her in his arms was so wonderful, her scent so sweet. It was like awakening from a nightmare and discovering the sun shining and world really all right.

"What about the annulment?" she said.

"What about it?"

"Don't you want it?"

Nick smiled and tweaked her nose. "That was just a ploy."

"A ploy for what?"

"To see if you really loved me. When you didn't object, I thought you were glad."

"Nick," she said, taking his face in her hands, "I was dying! You didn't ask me if I wanted an annulment, you told me you were getting one! I thought that's what you wanted."

He shook his head, tears bubbling from his eyes. "I guess we've both been fools." Then he laughed. "A couple of hardheaded Sicilians."

Felicia kissed him, and he kissed her back. He felt her heart pounding with excitement. His was, too.

"My God," he said, pressing his forehead against hers. "I'd given up hope."

Felicia nodded, brushing a tear from his cheek and one from hers. "Me, too."

Nick took the paper with the pregnancy test results from her hand and studied it. Then a dark look came over his face.

"What's the matter?" she asked.

"Felicia, what if the test had been negative?"

She shrugged. "What if it had?"

"Would you be here now? Would you have come to New York?"

"Nick, what are you asking? If I really want you, or if I'm just sticking with you because I'm needy and with child?"

"It's not an unreasonable question."

She laughed.

"What's so funny?"

"There's no way you'll ever be sure, is there?"

"Hey, that's not fair," he protested. "It's a very serious question."

"Is it?"

His expression softened to a smile. "Wouldn't you wonder, if you were in my shoes?"

Felicia kissed his chin. "Sometimes, sweetheart, life just isn't fair. Take it from someone who knows."

# Epilogue

NICK GLANCED out the taxi window as they made their way south on Seventh Avenue. It was an unusually warm April evening. Louisa, who sat between him and Carlo, dabbed her brow with her hanky.

"No disrespect to either of you," she said, "but this heat is reason enough to live in San Francisco."

"You get used to it," Nick said. "Felicia doesn't mind at all now."

"Felicia's a new bride and an expectant mother," Louisa said. "In a few years, she'll have you moving to San Francisco, mark my words."

"We'll see."

"The cool San Francisco fog is in my bones," Carlo said wistfully, "but to be here in New York is to be a young man again."

"Holy Mother," Louisa said, "don't tell me you'll want to move here, too."

"To be near my grandson, why not?"

"We'll discuss this some other time, Carlo," his wife said. "Our son-in-law does not want to hear us arguing about weather. He is concerned about Felicia, as we should be."

"Felicia's fine. Except that she's been on pins and needles for weeks," Nick said.

"About the restaurant or the baby?" Louisa asked.

"To be honest, I think she's more uptight about her dessert diner than the baby."

"She's her father's daughter all right," Louisa moaned. "The night I went into labor with Felicia, Carlo wanted to swing by the restaurant to make sure they hadn't run out of shrimp for the scampi special."

"Giving birth to this restaurant has been harder than what the baby will be, I'm sure," Nick said. "Thank God the grand opening is coming before her due date. I don't know what she'd have done if she'd gone into labor early."

"Probably have the doctor come to the restaurant," Louisa said.

They entered Greenwich Village. Carlo leaned forward for a better look. "This could be San Francisco," he said.

"I think it was one reason Felicia picked it. She liked Sheridan Square because of all the theater traffic."

"Location is very important," Carlo said. "Second only to the food and the service."

Nick had to smile. He recalled a conversation when Felicia had anguished over where to put her restaurant. She'd liked the idea of the off-Broadway theater district. "People are hungry after they've seen a good show, just like after good sex," she'd said.

He had to acknowledge the wisdom of that insight. The past seven months had been the most idyllic of his life. Felicia had brought him great joy. Not only was the sex good, but their love for each other seemed boundless. And the food he got wasn't bad.

In preparation for the opening of her dessert diner, Nick had been her guinea pig. He'd gained nearly ten pounds, but it had been a heavenly way to go. "Once I've got the diner open, we'll go on diets," she said. "I'll have thirty pounds to lose."

"Yes, but you'll be able to drop a lot of it in one day."

They had laughed, as they did much of the time. Their only less than joyful time had been the day of Uncle Vinny's funeral. Felicia had gone out of respect to Maria. "Your uncle caused me much suffering," she said, "but where would I be now without him? Probably still a spinster, dreaming about opening a dessert diner one day."

When the taxi pulled up in front of Just Desserts, Nick got out, paid the driver, then helped Louisa and Nick from the cab. The Mauros stared at the front of the diner with the huge banner reading Grand Opening.

"I'm so damned proud," Carlo said, wiping a tear from his eye. "I can't tell you how grateful I am, Nick, for giving my angel her dream."

"Don't thank me. Felicia did this herself. I helped a little with the real estate part of it, but that's all."

"I don't just mean the dessert diner," Carlo said, throwing an arm around Nick's shoulder. "Thank you for loving her. She deserves it more than anybody who ever lived."

"You don't have to tell me that, Pops," Nick said with a wink. "Every day I thank my lucky stars that you and Vinny met, difficult as it's been for you."

"Maybe this proves even a little good can come out of evil. I hope so. Otherwise, sinners couldn't go on living."

"Enough about sin, Carlo Mauro," Louisa said. "This is Felicia's happy day. Come on, let's go in."

They went inside. Felicia had gathered the staff together for a last-minute pep talk before they officially opened. Nick and her parents waited near the door. After sending everyone off to work, she came over to them, her beautiful face rounder than before and glowing with joy.

"Mama, Pops," she said, kissing her parents. Then she turned to Nick. "Thanks for bringing them, darling." She gave him a kiss.

"Felicia, this is wonderful," Carlo said, then wandered off to check the place out.

She had gone with the Italian espresso bar look. Everything was modern with lots of chrome and glass. There were only twelve tables, though there were six stools at the bar to take care of additional patrons. Half a dozen people were gathered outside to look at the menu.

She smiled at Nick, giving an exhausted sigh.

"How you holding up?" he asked, putting an arm around her distended waist.

"Fine," she said.

Nick heard the word, but for some reason he didn't completely believe her. "Sure?"

"I couldn't be happier."

He noticed a fine sheen of perspiration on her lip. Just then she flinched.

"Felicia," he said, "are you all right?"

"Your son is eager for this show to get on the road. He's been kicking me like crazy the last few hours."

Nick ran his fingers over her fiery cheek. "Which show are we talking about?"

Felicia shrugged.

He took her by the shoulders. "Mrs. Mondavi, have you been having contractions?"

She gave him a woebegone look.

"I'm taking you to the hospital."

"No, Nick, please. They're only teeny tiny contractions. I've got to see my restaurant open."

"Oliver's ready to take over," Nick said. "That was our deal, remember? You hired someone you could trust to run things until you were ready to come to work. Your father's restaurant did just fine while he was recovering from his heart attack, don't forget."

"I know, Nick, but his place was established."

"If this place flops, we open another," he rejoined.

"Just let me have a couple of hours. Please."

He shook his head with dismay, but he wasn't really upset. He could tell she was determined. "Under one condition. That I have a taxi sitting out front on standby."

"Deal."

They embraced. Nick lifted her chin and kissed her lips.

"You make every major event in my life memorable," he said, "I'll give you that."

"Well, you've been the reason for every major event in my life," she said.

"Is that calculated to calm my wary heart?"

"Maybe."

He put his arm around her as they watched her parents wandering around, checking everything out.

"Remember the day of my hearing last October?" he said.

"You mean the one where we didn't know whether we'd be spending the rest of our lives in Italy or America?"

"That's the one."

"What about it?"

"You said you were going to keep me guessing as to whether you were staying with me because you were pregnant and needed a father for your child."

"Yeah, I remember. What about it?"

"Don't you think it's time you tell me?"

Felicia gave him a smile. "All right. I guess I owe you that. I definitely did not want to stay with you because of the baby. We could have gotten along without you okay."

Nick smiled broadly. "Then it *was* because you loved me."

She didn't say anything.

"Felicia?"

"Well, I'd given back your uncle's check. How in the world did you think I'd get my dessert diner without a sugar daddy to bankroll me?"

His mouth dropped open. At first he was shocked. Then, when she broke into gales of laughter, Nick realized she was teasing him. Again.

"I hate it when you do that," he said. "I fall for it every time."

"I don't know why you're so surprised, my love. In the end, everyone gets their just deserts."

*Just Desserts Just For You!*

## CHOCOLATE MOUSSE

| 11 oz | *bittersweet or semisweet chocolate* |
| ½ lb | *sweet butter* |
| 6 | *eggs* |

Cut chocolate into pieces and melt in a double boiler over hot water. While chocolate is melting, add butter, also cut into pieces. Stir until both are well mixed.

Remove from heat. Separate yolks from whites. Beat yolks briefly and add slowly to chocolate mixture. Put this mixture in the fridge for about 15 minutes. In the meantime, beat the whites into soft peaks.

Fold cooled chocolate mixture into whites till blended. (Don't overmix.) The whites will fall somewhat and the result will be a medium-brown, very soft mixture. Spoon into individual serving dishes, and refrigerate at least 4 hours, or until set. (The mousse darkens to a deep brown while setting.)

*Just Desserts Just For You!*

## ITALIAN COCONUT WEDDING CAKE

| | |
|---|---|
| Cream: | *2 cups sugar*<br>*1 stick butter*<br>*½ cup Crisco*<br>*5 egg yolks, beaten* |
| Sift 3 times: | *1 tsp baking soda*<br>*2 cups flour*<br>*½ tsp salt* |
| Add: | *1 cup buttermilk to the flour mixture, then add to creamed mixture.* |
| Then add: | *1 cup finely chopped pecans (or walnuts)*<br>*2 cups flaked coconut*<br>*1 tsp vanilla* |
| Beat: | *5 egg whites until stiff. Gently fold into batter. Divide into 3 round greased and floured pans. Bake at 350° for 30-35 minutes.* |
| Icing: | *⅔ stick margarine*<br>*8 oz cream cheese*<br>*1 box powdered sugar*<br>*1 tsp vanilla*<br>*¼ tsp salt* |

To make the icing, combine margarine and softened cream cheese in food processor. Add remaining ingredients and beat until smooth. Ice cooled layers (between the layers only—it's a torte). Sprinkle additional coconut between layers and on top of cake.

# *Just Desserts Just For You!*

## CHOCOLATE CREAM CHEESE BROWNIES

Preheat oven to 350° and grease a 9 x 12 pan.

| Chocolate Mixture: | *1 cup unsifted flour* |
| | *1 tsp baking powder* |
| | *½ tsp salt* |
| | *8 oz semisweet chocolate* |
| | *6 tbsp unsalted butter* |
| | *4 eggs* |
| | *1½ cups sugar* |
| | *2 tsp vanilla* |
| | *6-8 oz chopped pecans (or walnuts)* |

Sift together flour, baking powder and salt, then set aside. Melt together the butter and chocolate and let cool.

Beat eggs until foamy. Add sugar and vanilla and beat on high for 3-4 minutes. Then on low add chocolate mixture and dry ingredients, using a spatula to thoroughly mix. Remove and set aside 1½ cups of this mixture. Add nuts to remaining mixture and spread in prepared pan.

| Cheese Mixture: | *12 oz cream cheese* |
| | *6 tbsp butter* |
| | *2 tbsp vanilla* |
| | *¾ cup sugar* |
| | *3 eggs* |

Beat together butter and cream cheese until soft and smooth. Add vanilla and sugar and beat well. Add eggs and beat again until smooth. Pour over chocolate layer. Then drop big spoonfuls of the reserved chocolate mixture over the cream cheese mixture and swirl with a knife to marbleize the batter. Bake for 40-45 minutes. When completely cooled, cut into squares and refrigerate.

**HARLEQUIN® Temptation**

## MEN OF WHISKEY RIVER

### Three sexy, unforgettable men
### Three beautiful and *unusual* women

Come to Whiskey River, Arizona, a place "where anything can happen. And often does," says bestselling author JoAnn Ross of her new Temptation miniseries. "I envision Whiskey River as a romantic, magical place. A town like Brigadoon, hidden in the mists, just waiting to be discovered."

Enjoy three very *magical* romances.

#605 *Untamed* (Oct.)

#609 *Wanted!* (Nov.)

#613 *Ambushed* (Dec.)

**Come and be spellbound**

# Take 4 bestselling love stories FREE

## Plus get a FREE surprise gift!

## Special Limited-time Offer

**Mail to Harlequin Reader Service®**

3010 Walden Avenue
P.O. Box 1867
Buffalo, N.Y. 14240-1867

**YES!** Please send me 4 free Harlequin Temptation® novels and my free surprise gift. Then send me 4 brand-new novels every month, which I will receive before they appear in bookstores. Bill me at the low price of $2.90 each plus 25¢ delivery and applicable sales tax, if any.* That's the complete price and a savings of over 10% off the cover prices—quite a bargain! I understand that accepting the books and gift places me under no obligation ever to buy any books. I can always return a shipment and cancel at any time. Even if I never buy another book from Harlequin, the 4 free books and the surprise gift are mine to keep forever.

142 BPA A3UP

| Name | (PLEASE PRINT) | |
|---|---|---|
| Address | Apt. No. | |
| City | State | Zip |

This offer is limited to one order per household and not valid to present Harlequin Temptation® subscribers. *Terms and prices are subject to change without notice. Sales tax applicable in N.Y.

UTEMP-696

©1990 Harlequin Enterprises Limited

# #610 A MAN FROM OKLAHOMA
## by Lisa Harris

Meet Jake Good Thunder. Half-Sioux, half-Irish, he's one hundred percent rogue. As an undercover vice cop, he's used to playing with fire. But when his old flame, gorgeous Julie Fitzjames, comes to him, desperately needing his help, he knows he's going to get burned....

All men are not created equal. Some are rough around the edges. Tough-minded but tenderhearted. Incredibly sexy. The tempting fulfillment of every woman's fantasy.

When it's time to fight for what they believe in, to win that special woman, our Rebels and Rogues are heroes at heart.

**Watch for A MAN FROM OKLAHOMA in November, wherever Harlequin books are sold.**

Look us up on-line at: http://www.romance.net

REBELS10/96

As Seen on TV!

# Free Gift Offer

With a Free Gift proof-of-purchase
from any Harlequin® book, you can receive
a beautiful cubic zirconia pendant.

This stunning marquise-shaped stone is a genuine cubic
zirconia—accented by an 18" gold tone necklace.
(Approximate retail value $19.95)

## Send for yours today...
## compliments of ◈ HARLEQUIN®

To receive your free gift, a cubic zirconia pendant, send us one original proof-of-purchase, photocopies not accepted, from the back of any Harlequin Romance®, Harlequin Presents®, Harlequin Temptation®, Harlequin Superromance®, Harlequin Intrigue®, Harlequin American Romance®, or Harlequin Historicals® title available in August, September or October at your favorite retail outlet, together with the Free Gift Certificate, plus a check or money order for $1.65 U.S./$2.15 CAN. (do not send cash) to cover postage and handling, payable to Harlequin Free Gift Offer. We will send you the specified gift. Allow 6 to 8 weeks for delivery. Offer good until December 31, 1996, or while quantities last. Offer valid in the U.S. and Canada only.

# Free Gift Certificate

Name: _____

Address: _____

City: _____ State/Province: _____ Zip/Postal Code: _____

Mail this certificate, one proof-of-purchase and a check or money order for postage and handling to: HARLEQUIN FREE GIFT OFFER 1996. In the U.S.: 3010 Walden Avenue, P.O. Box 9071, Buffalo NY 14269-9057. In Canada: P.O. Box 604, Fort Erie, Ontario L2Z 5X3.

---

## FREE GIFT OFFER

084-KMFR

ONE PROOF-OF-PURCHASE

To collect your fabulous FREE GIFT, a cubic zirconia pendant, you must include this original proof-of-purchase for each gift with the properly completed Free Gift Certificate.

---

084-KMFR

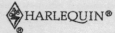

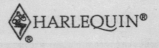